Ditch

Ditch

Hal Niedzviecki

a novel

Random House Canada

National Library of Canada Cataloguing in Publication Data

Niedzviecki, Hal, 1971–
   Ditch : a novel

ISBN 0-679-31110-6

I. Title.

PS8577.I3635D57 2001   C813'.54   C2001-930125-1
PR9199.3.N53D57 2001

www.randomhouse.ca

Text design: Daniel Cullen

Printed and bound in Canada

10 9 8 7 6 5 4 3 2 1

For Rachel Greenbaum and
Nina Niedzviecki

1

I didn't even lie, Debs thinks, her eyes skipping along the walls.

She runs her finger across the top of the refrigerator. A grey smear obscuring her print. She could be anywhere. She could be anyone.

She didn't fill out any forms, answer any questions, submit to a credit check, make up references, a history.

Debs hasn't ever wanted anything. The empty space of longing inside her, a coffin, a secret buried in the earth of her flesh. She has the drifter's terror of greeting the familiar, of staying in one place too long.

"Mom?"

She isn't home yet. She's still at work. Ditch is just checking.

He squints. The muddled shape of his jacket slumped into itself. Everything seems outlined, grey, even the light coming under the crack of the door. Too thick. Too dark.

It's this house, he thinks. The moment lingers, unresolved, falling over the abstracted patterns of a coat's folds. He doesn't want to have to think. You're always dreaming, his mother complains. He's twenty-three years old, he goes to work, he comes home, he sticks his tongue out at himself in the mirror — an invisible blur, an empty space reflecting nothing; he sees a face he recognizes; he sees this hallway, the house he's been living in all his life. She wants him to go to college. She wants him to grow up. He's a virgin.

He kicks the jacket. He kicks it again. He sends it skittering into the corner of the vestibule. The jacket puts up no resistance. It crumbles into itself — clothes bought sizes too big, garments folded in over themselves, don't worry, you'll grow into it.

"Mom?"

He blinks, gropes for the light switch.

She's not home yet. He shakes off his boots. A visible odour rises like steam from the damp lining. His feet stick against the walls of his socks. He looks for somewhere to put his boots. His mother hates his boots. What can he do? You wear a pair of boots five days a week, there gets to be an odour. He doesn't know where to put the boots. He could put them in the front foyer, just a dark hallway, the door to their apartment, the stairs leading up to Knudtsen's. But she'd smell them. She'd open the front door and smell them. They remind me of your father, she'd say. What about him? he wants to ask her.

Ditch sweats. Turns away from his boots, his shapeless coat, leaves the familiar objects where they land. He can never decide where to put things. He shuffles through the dim hall to his room. As he moves, he pulls his sweater over his head. He stops, halfway between one place and another, his face pressed against wool, his eyes straining into the moist space where fibres separate. What keeps things together? He can't see. He can't breathe.

The sweater gets stuck at his nose. He thrusts his arms straight up, swings left, then right. The apartment suddenly goes loud, his chest swelling in amplified heartbeats. He gets to his room, turns on the radio. A song, some vague jingle. Ditch pulls off his socks, falls backwards on his bed — legs in the air, he yanks his jeans off. The songs parade past, indifferent, a group of acquaintances nodding.

Into the bathroom, the cracks in the blue ceiling where tiles meet each other. Light streams through, the back window catching the fall sunset. Afternoon joins evening in a rustle of leaves. Before the steam from the shower layers over the tiny window, Ditch stands on his toes and sees the rusty barbecue, the abandoned bicycle, the snow shovel propped up against the side of the house. Steam makes things soft. The sound of the radio dank and dislocated.

In the shower Ditch is all straining ridges, hard crests and taut escarpments. He's got his eyes shut. He's got himself in a fist. One hand tightens around the shower curtain rod. His knees bend. He leans into his body, his body is nothing, all his weight down there in the rigid centre. His legs flex low, his arm holds the bar, swaying with the moment. The shower beats water against the green enamel of the tub. Drops scurry down the drain. Soap and steam, the give and take of need, this physical truth, this emptiness. A little lower, knees pointed up, feet almost not touching the tub, weight on that one hand-swinging arm.

He falls over the edge of the tub, his body. The curtain rod, ripped out of the wall, lands in a clatter. Sprawled around the toilet, reeling from the impact of the tiles against his forehead, Ditch shoots forward a giant, irrepressible gob. Hot water runs down the drain in streams. The plastic curtain lies under the sink. A wet-heaped moment.

"Hello," his mother calls. "Is anybody home?"

Barbara doesn't say anything about the bathroom. She's used to cleaning up. They meet in the kitchen. Her eyes trail down the flat plain of her son's body. "I don't feel like cooking tonight. Let's go out." She sighs, short of breath, the apartment torrid and gloomy, closing in. Ditch stands next to her, a gangly awkward man, a coat-hanger wrapped in jeans and a t-shirt. He looks down at the linoleum. The room is sloping, pressing the two of them together, against each other. Mother and son, parent and child.

His face is still red, the blush blooming over his cheeks and forehead.

"Mom, I —"

"How about Chinese?" Barbara says. "I'm starving. What a busy day. Didn't even have time for lunch. Christmas coming up, can you believe it? All the invites have to go out, it's busy non-stop."

Barbara works as a social coordinator, knows how to be correct, knows when to smooth things over. There's a space between people who love each other. The distance of intimacy, the cautious irony of blood. Ditch doesn't know about family. He doesn't think he has a family. The air in the apartment is laced with a dampness, an undercurrent that just catches in the hair of his nose, invisible particles penetrating, folding darkness into darkness.

Barbara shuts her eyes, presses her hands over her face. She wilts, grabs for the smooth edge of the counter, holds on.

"Hey, Mom, you okay?"

"Well," Barbara laughs, still gripping with white hands. "It's nothing. Working too hard. Just felt a little..."

For a moment she's a little girl again, lingering in the shadow of perpetual sunshine, a chasm splitting open and consuming

everything, a mother and child standing in a shaking doorway. It's still her greatest fear: order decimated, people lost
and never found, pictures shattering off walls, parties
rescheduled.

"C'mon, Mom. There's never been an earthquake in
Toronto."

"I know." She laughs. "But you never know."

But back then, wasn't that what she wanted? His father was
hitchhiking. She was working in a diner in California. Life
seemed possible, dangerous, unstable. She took pity on him,
gave the man who was to be her husband a free bowl of soup.
Fault lines crossing under nowhere crossroads. They married.
They moved. He wanted her to see it. His city. *Been here ever
since*, she tells her co-workers over lunch, the words coming
out of her mouth like a good deed done by accident.

Ditch feels his stomach tighten. A hardening inside him.
The thick part of a flat belly. The space between them, splitting.

"Chinese," Barbara says. She has a lipstick out, a tiny mirror.
"Let's go right now. I'm starved. I won't even get changed." She
bulges her lips, applies colour. They stand still, the heavy air
around them, Barbara breathing it in too fast, Ditch tasting his
own embarrassment.

He turns and walks down the hall. His coat hangs in the
closet. He doesn't see his boots. He can't smell them. His
mother beside him. The hard shield of his stomach, fists
curled, he's angry again. Not at his mother, not at the shrink-
ing gloom of the apartment; after all, she does her best for
him. He catches his face in the mirror, turning away. It's the

way she walks, her back rigid and straight, prepared to face any adversity, that string of miniature earthquakes threatening to break like indiscreet revelations.

"Where are my —?"

"I just put them in that old bag in the closet there, that old silver plastic bag."

Ditch drags his boots out of the bag.

"Why do you —?" he starts to say.

Instead, he falls back to a sitting position on the floor and pulls them on. His mother inspects herself in the mirror.

Ditch drives, hunched over the steering wheel. He has his eyes closed. He sees the route: houses, parks, highways, strip malls, schools.

He smells of fresh ink on newsprint, a sour dry pressing.

The route is a picture. The bluish haze of sky against eyelids. He keeps his eyes closed, has to keep his eyes closed. How do we know we are where we are? Thinking about things until everything is image, nothing is real. The van sways, tires squeal, Ditch holds on, his fingers against the hard plastic of the steering wheel.

He opens his eyes.

The bright blue sky pours a waterfall.

He's on the expressway, heading toward the western suburbs. It's his favourite part of the route, just before Mississauga. He can see the river winding down to Lake Ontario, the leaves shimmering red and yellow and brown. His face is turned to the side window as he accelerates, the van balanced for a half second on two wheels then dropping down to four.

"It's nothing," Ditch says. The urge to keep his eyes closed. Distance like a lurid memory. "I'm just tired."

Ditch talks to himself when he drives. It's normal. He's lonely. Six hours, eight hours, the time passes like scenery. It's nothing. Just a few words here and there. A sentence. Never in public. He tries not to in public.

He pulls up to the strip mall: quickie mart, dollar store, save-a-centre groceries, pharma-plus, donut emporium with a sign in the window: *bathroom customer only*. Ditch opens his door and jumps down. He stumbles almost falling. The still movement of the van turning revolutions. His legs are rubbery. No, not his legs but the muscles of his legs; they're asleep, Ditch thinks, but it's more like an itch, a permeating rash spreading down the inside slopes of his bony thighs.

He goes in.

"Hi there," Carla says, smiling. Ditch nods to the Good Time Donuts and Deli team. Carla and Bill. Carla hands him a coffee.

All day, Ditch thinks. Every day.

"The usual?" Carla smiles. They wear matching t-shirts, Carla and Bill. Carla's seems a bit tighter than Bill's. Carla is older than Ditch, but younger than his mother. Ditch raises his chin to look at her face fringed in a shoulder-length frost of blonde hair. Suddenly, violently, he lowers his gaze. Behind him, the regulars smoke, plumes of feathered grey spreading out over the tops of newspapers.

"The usual," Carla decides, raising her voice as if Bill is a dog who only responds to a certain pitch.

"Right," Bill says. "With pickles, right?"

"Yes, Bill," Carla says patiently. Ditch feels the itch in his legs. When the usual comes — a western sandwich garnished with lettuce, tomato and pickle — he chews it mechanically, the taste of shrimp and noodles coated in rich brown sauce lingering in some dark crevice under his tongue.

"I didn't order this," he says.

Slumped in the driver's seat again, the landscape blurring by, Ditch wishes he could do something with his legs. He pulls the window down, breathes deep. The van reels out onto the 427, swerving suddenly in another direction.

"Shit," he mutters. Brake lights and bumpers. "Must be an accident." He fiddles with the radio, inches the van along, traffic stopped all the way past the airport — like always, he thinks, pressing the soles of his boots against the bevelled bottom of the van. Above him, planes lurch into the clear sky. Ditch thinks about the donut girl. Carla. She's old. He follows the streaks of dispersing exhaust through the atmosphere. She's old. She's probably thirty. She works in the donut store. With Bill.

Ditch nudges the van forward. Fills the space left open to him. Sometimes they try to cut in. They come in from the lane that's ending and they try to cut in.

Ditch rolls the window all the way down, leans into the scoured taste, the layer of exhaust on his tongue a hot milk skin.

The highway skims the tops of factories, warehouses, industrial complexes, superstore outlets. All the buildings, grey monoliths subsumed by the perfect expanse of sky. Ditch keeps his face out, breathing, trying not to think about breathing.

"Chinese," he says to the gritty wind. "Chinese with Mom."

Finally, he merges with the 401. Traffic picks up. Twenty minutes later, he's in Scarborough, working his way over to University of Toronto's suburban campus. He'll drop off a load of newspapers and pick up last week's load, a similar stack. Untouched, unread. The wide streets, the tree-lined avenues, huge houses with thick white doors. It's Friday. He feels his long legs compressed. Tonight, he thinks. He's invited to a party. The waitress at the bar he sometimes goes to. Suzie. He thinks she might be beautiful. The place is a dive. He goes there because nobody ever goes there. She works there for the same reason. She invited him.

He waits at a light. A skinny woman wrapped in a bathrobe wanders aimlessly to the foot of her driveway then turns abruptly and half-runs back to her open front door. It must be nice, Ditch thinks. When the light changes he makes a left. "Here it comes," he says to himself. "The private school." He pumps the brakes as if feeling for something. The van is barely moving. I won't look, Ditch thinks. But it's bright out and it's lunchtime and all the girls are out front, smoking cigarettes and staring defiantly at the slowing traffic. Ditch turns his head as the van drifts by. The girls purse their lips to pull in smoke, legs jut out of their plaid skirts like toothpicks. He isn't looking.

Ditch walks to the kitchen, naked feet trailing little puddles. His mom's working late tonight — *functions* — that's what she calls them. He imagines her smile, bright and polite, hands pressing into hands, a certain smug dryness, a certain arrangement of seating. Her voice delivered like the weather.

He stops in front of the refrigerator. The towel hangs like a shawl around his shoulders. He takes out the orange juice carton and unscrews the cap. He stands by the fridge with the bright plastic cap loose in his palm. He tilts the carton, fills his mouth with juice. He forgets to swallow until he feels the cold trickle down his chin. Then he gulps the juice down, gasps for air. He puts the carton back in the refrigerator. He wipes his face with his arm. The orange cap still in his hand. He slams the refrigerator door shut. His mother's note flaps under its magnet mooring:

"Ditch, honey. Please go up and see Mr. Knudtsen. I promised to visit him tonight, but I forgot I had a function. Make sure that he is okay and ask him if he needs anything. Have you given any more thought to your future? Sandwich stuff in the fridge. I will be home late. Love, Mom."

Knudtsen rents the upstairs apartment. He's lived up there since Ditch was a little boy, that is, since before he could remember much of anything. Knudtsen joins them for birthdays and holidays. He used to be a tailor. Barbara calls him family. For Ditch the idea is exotic; the notion that he has a family. He keeps having this dream: hundreds of people are stuck waist-deep in the newspaper recycling dump. They don't struggle. They stand with their backs to Ditch and his van full of papers, waiting for him to unload over them. Family.

He opens the refrigerator again. Peers in, seeking something in the cold shadowed corners; a feeling he has. Hunger or something else. Knudtsen up there. Getting older. Ditch has a party to go to.

In Ditch's hand the note crumples against the plastic orange juice cap. He throws them both in the garbage under the sink.

Their house, jammed in between two others built to last in the nineteen-thirties, doesn't let much light in on the main floor. Ditch blinks, always unprepared for Knudtsen's suddenly bright upstairs apartment. The setting sun pours through the large window of the living room, a yolk yellow sticking to everything.

"How you keeping, my boy?" Knudtsen asks. His voice like gravel.

"Oh, fine," Ditch says, standing in the middle of the room, still squinting, smelling the old man smell. He looks at his watch. "Mom sent me, she can't make it, she's working tonight. So I'm here to, uh, you know, say hello."

Knudtsen laughs like a throat clearing. "Sit down, my boy. Sit anywhere."

Ditch perches himself on the edge of the red couch. Dust jumps up in spumes, catches in the glowing embers of dusk. The sun just above thick grey clouds. With spots still in his eyes, Ditch stares at Knudtsen, sitting in the armchair, a blanket over his knees. He looks away and then looks again, following the creviced cheeks, grooves forking and meeting like country roads. He feels a warmth in his chest, the lingering conscience of bodies — so alive and possible.

"You sitting or standing?" Knudtsen asks. He shields his eyes from the sun. It doesn't matter. He can't see that far. He's going blind.

"I'm sitting," Ditch says. He says it again: "I'm sitting." The couch is a rock under him.

"Never mind," says Knudtsen, suddenly, waving a dismissing limb. "A young man like you, so much to do, so much to do. I had better to do once, I know about it. You're working?"

"Yes."

"Helping your mother?"

"Yes."

"A good woman."

"She wanted me to tell you she'll see you on the weekend."

"On the weekend..." Knudtsen screws up his forehead. A maze. A puzzle.

"It's Friday. Friday night."

"Is it, now?"

"I'm going to a party," Ditch announces. He cringes, feels his face go hot. Why tell the old man that? Knudtsen is guilt and dreams and the solace of nostalgia. Family?

"You got a girl?" Knudtsen asks, crooked grin.

Ditch looks at his hands, the grooves of his fingers, the cuts where the sharp plastic bundling cords slide under his skin. Knudtsen leans into the downturned folds of his face. Ditch strokes the fabric of the couch, watches the faded red turn dark as it ruffles. He keeps his knees together, resists the urge to leap to his feet, pace around the room, stare out at the street Knudtsen can no longer see.

"You need anything?"

Knudtsen shakes his head.

"You got a girl? Tell an old man something." Knudtsen's lips still moving, the aftershock of remembered speech. "Tell me...what's it like...what's it like with the girls?"

Ditch turns, stealing a quick look at the street. How much time has passed? It's suddenly gloomy in the apartment, the sun falling under the clouds, disappearing; outside, he can see the trees dropping leaves, spiralling shadows making halos in the light of the street lamp. And it looks cold, he thinks. Almost winter. He presses his feet to the floor, toes flat, muscles stretching. A date tonight. He's nervous, isn't sure how it happened, how things happen. Why should he be nervous? Is it late? It's getting late.

Knudtsen makes that noise again, laughing, throat clearing, strangling.

"What's it like?"

"Well," Ditch says. "It's like, it's, you know, it's...the same."

"The same?"

"Well, you know..." Ditch says. A terrible itch in his legs.

"I haven't been out in weeks. Weeks. They cut my ride program. Bastards."

"They cut your program?"

"They used to come pick me up. I'd go to the Golden Age to play cards or see the concert, they always do a concert in the fall. I used to go, you know."

Dust creeps into Ditch's nose. "I'll take you, you tell me when it is and I'll take you over. We can use the van from work. I can get it any time. I have it tonight. It doesn't matter. No one cares. I can take you."

"Not tonight." Knudtsen laughs, coughs into a slack fist. "Don't even worry about me. Worry about the girls."

"No, really," Ditch says, getting up. "I will. You just tell me when it is, or tell Mom. I've got to go now. But you let me know any time."

"Take care of your mother," Knudtsen says, his eyes turning bright. "She's a beauty." Knudtsen coughs again, a fine mist spraying into his lap. "A lovely."

Ditch goes back to the refrigerator. He holds a jar of olives in his hand. Shrivelled green orbs, red pimento pushing through, a withered pregnancy. The old man loves her, he thinks. He puts the jar back.

Outside, a horn sounds hard edges through shadows. The deep urgency of an engine turning against itself. Ditch, face in the fridge. The horn, louder, continuous, repeating. A car alarm. What can I eat? Eggs, butter, a can of tuna, she keeps her tuna in the fridge, all the crazy family he has, nothing here, nothing to eat. He'll leave a note: *Mom. No sandwich stuff. Gone out. Gone to a party. Be back late. Won't be back.*

Someone bangs on the door.

Ditch moves through the hallway, the light from the refrigerator spilling out behind him.

"Yes?"

The man is in a suit. He looks normal. Now it's really night, Ditch thinks, peering into the evening haze. Why is he so surprised? It's night and he's late.

"Is that your van?"

Ditch steps out onto the walk. The man moves around to the front of the van, stops at the hood.

"It's blocking the sidewalk," the man says. His lips shift when he talks. He's normal. Everything might just be normal. Ditch's t-shirt, for instance. Short sleeves. Pale arms in the pale street-lamp light. But it's too cold. Way too cold.

"What?"

"Didn't you hear me?"

"I —"

The man slaps the hood.

"It's blocking the sidewalk."

Ditch watches the stranger's hand disappear, white on white, imperfect shadows. Leaves rustle in the gutter. It's fall. It's winter. It's too late, or too early, she's waiting. I hope she's waiting.

"I was just —"

"I had to walk around."
Another ringing slap and the man spins away.

Ditch shrugs, swings into the soft sinking seat, settles back, feet working the pedals. The engine rumbles. The sound is familiar, an old man's snore. Bathurst Street breaks into view. Suddenly exhausted, he has to fight the urge to let his eyes close.

He pulls up to her house. He waits at the curb, not sure what to do. Honk the horn? Ring the bell? He should go in and get her. What's he thinking? Mom would be — horrified —

But before he has a chance, a whole crowd spills out. Suzie waves to him. A guy wearing a Maple Leafs baseball cap taps on the window. Ditch lowers it.

"Beer?" the guy offers. He holds up a bottle.

"That's Bobby," Suzie says, swinging into the passenger seat. Ditch grabs the bottle waving in front of his face.

"Thanks," he says.

He drinks, feels empty.

"My father was a drinker," he says to Suzie.

"Everyone get in," she yells, prying open the sliding side door.

He rolls the van around a curve. The shapes become people, screaming and slamming against the walls. A girlish giggle. Someone saying: "Fuck off up there..." Suzie has a bottle between her thighs. There's something on the radio. Ditch watches Suzie sing along, her face caught in the street lights. She looks happy. It's not a date. It still might be a date. *She's sitting next to me.* She squeezes his arm.

"So, how are you? I love parties."

Ditch drinks, spills beer down his shirt.

The party is in a warehouse transformed into a studio. Giant gashes — bleeding organ oils — hang off the brick walls. Ditch moves into their frames and stops. He doesn't get out much. He holds tight to the bottle of beer in his hand.

Strobes flicker high overhead like collapsing stars. Ditch can't see Suzie. The party is its own country, a crammed shape shifting and flexing. He stands at the border of that encompassing land, some invisible fence between him and undiscovered territory. He keeps pouring beer in oblong splashes down into the part of himself he thinks he might be able to fill. He's alone, staring at an orange swath of kidney sprayed over with a thin mist of lime green.

"Do you like them?"

Ditch turns. She's hazy in the swirling strobe of lights. He can't quite make her out. He squints through the gloom, falls into it, her hurt grey eyes all he can see. Thinks of Knudtsen, the way the world must look to him now. *Why think about — she's a —* He takes a deep breath. He could be in love, if he wanted to be. He quickly looks back at the kidney canvas.

"They're like getting stitches!" he yells.

He hears her laugh, a peal of bells so different from the repetitive pulse of the music.

He shifts his beer into his other hand and rubs his wet palm on the leg of his jeans.

"I'm...Ditch," he says. His paw waving. She giggles again, just touches the palm of his hand with her fingers. Cold and impossibly small.

"Debs," she says.

He thinks she might be shivering.

"You're cold?"

"It's snowing," she says. "I can't believe it."

The way she says it, like she really can't believe it.

"It's snowing?" Ditch repeats.

The canned beat of dance music.

"What?"

Ditch shrugs. Forget it. Her breath against the hot side of his face.

She steps back, looking at him as if from a distance. Ditch reaches into a trash can filled with ice and pulls out a bottle. He twists off the cap, points the beer at her. She drinks. Her throat lilts as she swallows.

"C'mon," he says. He holds on to her, finds the door, pulls them outside. She stands beside him, resting against the white wall of the van.

"This is fucking amazing," she says. "Snow."

Ditch tilts himself off the side.

Snow, I didn't even —

He holds his hand out, watches the tiny flakes disappear. He is anywhere the white flakes flutter out of the bottom of a coal night, the snow driven to land by the pushing lake wind. His head pounds to the beat of the music, he feels the ache in his legs, wants to run away, wants to wrap around her, disappear into her.

She's shivering again.

"Should I," he says, "I mean..."

She leans into him.

"I hope it snows forever," she says. "You know? It's so...and I'm...Where I come from...Listen to me. I don't even know what I'm talking about." She throws her bottle down the road. It skitters on a carpet of white, doesn't break. "You can kiss me, you know."

First snow always sticks, Ditch thinks.

Then Suzie is there, her warm bare arm around his shoulder like the press of a mother, hugging bones.

"Hey! I've been looking for you!"

Ditch nods. A thickness coming up his throat. Suzie next to him, beer tasting like regret — the grateful discovery of some unrequited kindness.

"Lame party," Suzie says. "So snobby. I guess it's some kind of art thing. All those gross pictures. I didn't know it was gonna be like this. But hey, the free beer's all right."

Ditch nods again. He wants to tell her. What can he say —

He stares down the road, imagines the distance.

I should go, he thinks. It's late. Mom'll be worried.

But he stays where he is, slumped against the beached side of the white van. Departure is a feeling. A fear in his legs, an aching. Long years repeating. Familiar seasons: the next year, the year after that.

He'll see her again. Has to.

It seems like he's always driving. The give and swing of the wet rubber treads spinning. The van keels, he feels it slipping sideways. He puts his hands against the thin sheet of the van's curved wall. He is the one drifting.

"All right!" Suzie yells as they slide into the skid. Her voice a dead echo. Ditch feels it too, the deflated optimism of an accident on purpose; adrenaline, futility, tires not quite gripping the road.

The people in the back of the van are limpid shapes, the beer bottles in their hands gleaming as street lighting brushes through the front window. Ditch sees Suzie in the rear-view mirror. Suzie and Bobby, their faces lit up. The dark flashing spaces between street lamps, people, possibilities. Someone hooting. Ditch waits for those moments, fleeting clarity, he sees Bobby's hand on her sweater, he sees their lips moving, then Suzie's head disappears. Bobby's face in a peripatetic loll. His legs are out from under him. Someone laughing. When the light steeps in, Ditch can see her lips spread open.

Then Suzie starts screaming:

"You fuck. He puked. You asshole. You fucking fucker. You puked on my head."

Someone goes: "Stop the van. Stop the van."

They throw the back door open. Ditch has him by the ankles. Suzie has his arms. Suzie yells: "One, two, three." Ditch swings three times, lets go.

Ditch on the passenger side, his face rolling against the window. The van moving forward in soft gentle rhythms.

"Hey. Wake up."

Suzie claps her hands together.

"You're home."

I don't want to —

"Hey, you awake? Ditch? Are you okay? I'm sorry if — I never meant, you know? That asshole. I'm just going to park the van in front of your house here. You'll have to move it in the morning. I mean, you'll get a ticket. Here. Take the keys."

She kisses him quickly, on the cheek. He wants to say something, but can't seem to get the words out. I'm not drunk, he thinks.

She walks away, quickly.

Ditch stands still on the sidewalk. Arms wrapping the mist of snow around him.

He pulls at his boots, stumbles backwards into the closet. He falls down there in the vestibule dragging at a handful of laces, closing his eyes with his head against the soft wood of the door.

He wakes up with the dry taste of cotton in his mouth. Early morning light in soft dizzy fronds. The night through him, a sharp snowy turn. His stomach skids, he feels the clap of vomit on Suzie's head, the damp yielding skin of Bobby's wrists. One. Two. Three. Ditch pulls himself up and swamps into the bathroom. He throws up in the sink.

His mother in her robe, dark green velour, a cord tied around her waist, her hands in the pockets.

Ditch wipes his face on the arm of his jacket.

"You left the fridge open," Barbara says.

He runs the tap. Swirls cold water in his mouth, spits. He fumbles to turn the water off.

"Wash your face," Barbara says. "At least wash your face."

His legs burn. He's afraid to close his eyes. He pushes past his mother and into the hall. He breathes.

"You're just like your father."

"No," he says. "I'm just. You don't, it's just that I'm...not feeling well."

"I know," Barbara says. Ditch leans toward her. She puts a hand on his caged chest, pushes him away. "I know what you feel," she says. Ditch thinks she might tell him. Her body quivers in her faded robe, her flesh loose and maternal, holding on, desperate to itself. Alone. I'm alone.

But then the tiny bathroom shakes, dust fading down from the ceiling, a giant crack spreading between them.

"Earthquake," Barbara whispers.

"The next bus? Please."

The ticket woman looks up at her. Debs presses against the counter, afraid of the downtown bus station, the loitering men, lumps sprawled out on the sidewalk, reaching out slowly, patiently, for her passing ankles. She puts her bag between her feet. The ticket woman's jowls shake.

"Where you going?"

"Somewhere far," Debs says.

The woman ducks behind her terminal.

"Cincinnati. Ten minutes."

Debs shakes her head.

The woman smiles. "Don't want to go to Oh-hi-o?" She looks down at the terminal again. "Bus leaving for Buffalo, goes all the way to Toronto. That'll take you twenty-two hours, that one. Leaves in five minutes." The woman stares at Debs. "Four minutes now," she says. "I got cousins in Toronto."

"Where are you from?"

"Potomac, Maryland."

The customs guy studies her.

"What's your final destination?"

"Toronto."

"And the purpose of your visit?"

"I have cousins there."

She has no passport, no driver's licence, no birth certificate. She has nothing to show this man that she is who she says she is, attached to a country, a state, a city. Who is she? Her hands in her pockets. He doesn't ask. Doesn't seem to notice her lack of documents, the absence of luggage. She doesn't have a single bag. Just Daddy's laptop, the slick plastic casing cool against her hot hand. Memories or dreams. She closes her eyes, sees a box full of blood. On disc, on hard drive, there's a truth that beats like a heart, without waiting for permission. There's a kind of truth. I'm in some kind of trouble. Am I in some kind of trouble? She carries her body.

At the next booth a man in a dirty blue suit pleads in broken English.

The customs guy stamps the form, pushes it back to her, grinning. "Enjoy your stay."

Her fingers brush the top of his hand.

When she steps off the bus, she puts her hand in the pocket of her jeans and cups coins. Debs has American change and isn't even sure if she can use it in the pay phone. She looks around, as if for some sign of the strangeness of her new country. It's hotter than she thought it would be; Canada is supposed to be cold, but the people passing her on the dusty street in front of the bus terminal sport shorts, crumpled t-shirts dark at the armpits, their bodies hunched as if defeated by the hot humid press of the city sun. It's not what she expected. Summer in Canada. A couple walk by, nose rings and tank tops, but she doesn't have the courage to ask them: Is there even such a thing — Canadian money?

She puts a quarter in the pay phone. It falls through with a solid thunk. She looks down at the phone book. Her finger marks the number.

"Interlock Online," a man says.

"I need an account."

"She's bones now," Debs explains. "My mother."

Ditch stares at her; she's already perfect, already a picture in his memory.

"Nothing left," she sighs, looking around. "Any problems with mice or roaches?"

She pauses in front of the window. The red couch is gone, carried away with all the rest of Knudtsen's furniture. At the funeral Barbara buried her face in Ditch's shoulder. He stood suit straight. His hand on the back of her head. The emptiness surprised him. He's dead. She loved him. It doesn't matter. This old guy shows up. Knudtsen's brother. He doesn't cry or anything. Says he's the brother. Knudtsen's dead, Ditch thinks.

"You get a draft through this window?"

Ditch doesn't answer. She smiles, fidgets, puts her hands on her face.

"Hello? Mister?"

Mister, he thinks. She called me Mister.

She doesn't remember.

She fidgets, shifts, favours her left foot; it's barely noticeable. Ditch notices.

"If you want the place," he hears himself say, "it's yours."

Barbara stands outside the house. Late afternoon, night coming on. It's just past four-thirty. The wind. Down the street over clumped heaps of leaves and garbage. A new season hanging in the air. The grey smouldering remains of last week's early snow.

She puts a foot on the front step, then stops. She tips her head toward the second floor. *The light* —

Knudtsen's dead. So what if he is, she thinks. She hates to admit it, but it's like a release, the difference between looking through a window and opening it. It's for the best. The world goes on, changes, he was old — I'm getting — she's learned to accept change, the harsh painful clarity of it.

It's for the best. He didn't suffer.

You've got to move on: absence and guilt — sorrow — a new winter coming, or else, she thinks, it's already here, hanging in the air, waiting for us to notice it.

The light in the window flickers out. Barbara steps up to the door. She hears footsteps coming down and hurries to fit her key in the lock. She wants to meet Ditch in the foyer, the nothing space between the two apartments. Maybe, she thinks, he'd like to move up there, that way — he could — he's too old to live with his mother, if he pays some of the rent, sure, why not? She'll tell him, if he wants to, it's time he had his own place —

She'll grab hold of him and feel him against her. Anything else is hopeless.

She pushes the door open. Steps in. Warm musty air blows into her face, the stink of being alive, having a history, being in a place and learning to live in that place.

A wisp of a girl comes down the stairs. Slight, blonde, frantic. Half smiles at Barbara, skips out the door, disappears.

Ditch wakes up from the dream and sees his mother standing over him. The must of ink and newspaper clings to the wet part of his mind. A nightscape journey, a sleepwalk through Knudtsen's funeral and everything after that. *A beauty. A lovely.*

Barbara leans over, puts the grocery bags on the floor. Plastic creases fold like stiff hair. She stands up straight, crosses her arms over her chest. Ditch clings to his dream: holding his mother, feeling her cry, leaning over the sink and letting a mouthful of vomit spill out. In his dream, he directs hired men into Knudtsen's apartment, watches that old red couch disappear into the back of a truck. Past days. It all happened just like that, but, somehow, Ditch missed it, he wasn't really there. One thing after another, moments in a dream, nonsensical, inevitable. Knudtsen's stuff: a shuffled folder of grey photos; a pile of letters in another language.

The tight repression of her face. Her forehead a staircase of angry white lines. Ditch gets up out of the armchair. He plants his feet, his legs creeping up on him, itching.

"Outside, up there, there was a light, in Knudtsen's apartment —"

"He's gone," Ditch says.

"Ditch, I know that. Honey, don't you think I know that?"

Ditch nods. He isn't sure.

"I rented the upstairs."

The wisps of blonde falling down over her ears, she looked so fragile, her face tucked into that small body — and there was something else. Something.

"Ditch," she says. "You didn't rent the apartment to that girl. You didn't."

"She paid in cash."

"That's not the point! This is my house! My house. Do you understand me?"

"Don't yell," Ditch says.

Later she'll be alone, listening to herself. She'll play it back in her mind, cringe at the sound of her brittle anger, at the kind of things said through the drowning rescue of love.

Ditch stands. He looks at his mother. It's as if he's never seen her before. She's staying, he thinks. She's staying, she's staying, she's staying.

A single lamp is on in the living room. It's almost winter. It gets dark before they notice. People need to prepare. Otherwise, things happen without them noticing. A circle of light, a lamp, a living room.

Ditch lets his legs carry him.

Clubs, bars, restaurants. A door thudding shut. There's nothing stopping Ditch but the city. A sense of elsewhere, intangible charms, wasted dreams, spilled drinks. There's a bar, but lately — ever since, he hasn't been —

It's raining.

His legs push like a rash. He follows, then cuts up a side street of dark houses.

Walking west on Queen Street until Spadina. Wind sweeps through, catches the flapping corners of collars, blows bursts of rain hard against the sidewalk.

Ditch watches a woman in leather pants. She is holding on to a man and crying. Her makeup runs in streaks, the rain and the tears. She's my age, Ditch thinks. The man looks around, one arm awkwardly draped over her, the other waving toward the road. The man is older, could be her father, but isn't. Ditch thinks of her, sleeping on the floor, wrapped in a thin blanket. Sleeping on the floor of Knudtsen's apartment. Listening to the wind rattle against the big front window, feeling the hard wood against her hips, the solid comfort. Why isn't he with her? She doesn't know him. She doesn't remember the party. *You can kiss me, you know.* Why should she? I'm not — I'm just —

Lightning cracks and a burst of rain blinds him. Shrieks from the street. He takes shelter in the entrance to a bank. Her name is Debs, she smiles too much, her mother is dead. He doesn't know her.

He turns, his legs moving him down the block. A woman sits behind a large wooden crate. A blue plastic poncho tents over her torso. She is telling a drunk to go home. *Advice Lady* reads the scarlet letters carelessly splattered on the green painted plywood box. The drunk pushes off, reaching into his pocket and dropping a handful of change into the jar marked "tips." The woman plunks her elbows on the wood and sighs.

"Who's next?" she yells. Passersby quicken their steps. Ditch lurks in the shadows.

He feels his face go hot. His legs carry him.

"So what's your story?" Her voice an expression — the city filled with these loose smiles, impenetrable, the girl asleep, waking to the rumble of the streetcar, drawing the blanket around her.

"You do this every night?" Ditch asks.

She shrugs. "This is my last night for the season. Maybe forever."

"You make money doing this?"

A couple passing. The man says something in a loud whisper; the woman snickers. Ditch starts to get up.

"I was just," he says, testing his warm breath against the

hot flush of his face. "I was just, really not out tonight. Just going for a walk."

She nods, looking at him. "You should get out more."

"I guess. It's just that I was — thinking about my father. He left my mother when I was two years old."

"At least you got rid of the bum."

She laughs. Ditch stands up, his legs uncertain.

"That's what my mother says."

The woman laughs again, shrugs. "Your mother."

Ditch digs into the wet pocket of his jeans and pulls out his battered wallet — birthday gift from Mom when he turned seventeen. He tips the wallet and change pours out into his palm. A few laminated cards slip out of their loose pocket. He drops change in the tip jar, pays for something, feels like he should be paying for something. He kneels down, scrapes plastic off the sidewalk.

Someone standing above him. A hand on his damp long neck. Ditch looks up. It's Suzie. Her face is red from drinking and her hair is different, packed into a shiny shell.

"Hi, stranger. Remember me?" She smiles against the wind. "A little wet?"

Her eyes are wide, her mouth open.

Advice Lady laughs. "Get a room."

Suzie grabs his arm, pulls him along. She's wearing a gold top, some kind of velvet. It's wet. Her hair pressed against her forehead in a glamour-girl matte. She pulls her jean jacket around her and Ditch feels guilty.

"Lately," she laughs, "I keep running into people. Everywhere I go, I run into someone." She starts walking, swaying as she moves. Ditch steady at her side, like he's keeping her balance.

He sits down on a bulging pillow stuffed into a wicker chair. The walls of the living room are each painted a different colour: orange, green, purple, yellow.

The ceiling has clouds, blue, grey.

Debs.

"You ever think about going crazy?" Suzie calls from the kitchen.

"What?"

"Nothing."

She fills two short glasses. A bottle of something clear. She strikes a match. The lights go out.

"Hey," Ditch says. No windows, just the walls in nursery colours. Suzie appears, walking slowly. She puts the candle down on a stack of fashion magazines. The fire flickers. She raises her other hand to Ditch so that he can slide a glass out from between her fingers.

"I know," she said. "It's amazing. I'm amazing." She giggles. "Well, anyway, I'm a waitress."

Ditch raises his glass. Suzie tilts her head, drinks. She gasps, thin shoulders shaking.

"Terrible," she says. She laughs. "I try *not* to think about stuff like that." She looks at him. "But sometimes...I'm glad you're here. I'm sorry, I didn't mean — before — You're not drinking?"

His palms are wet. He raises the glass to his lips, coughs, forces the rest down. He feels his face turn red. He coughs again, tries to say something, the words catch. He looks down at his knees.

"You get used to it," Suzie says. She crouches on the floor in front of him. Her eyes shine. The candle shadows his stretched legs.

She puts her hand on his knee.

Debs, he thinks. He doesn't know what she looks like. He can picture her. He breathes in the air. Suzie jumps up from her squat. Her breasts shift under the gold top. The back of the van, street lights blasting through, lips stretched, neck stuttering. Lump in his throat. Ditch adjusts himself against his jeans. Suzie spins around. A lock of her hair escapes from its crafted shell. It curls down her forehead, a brown trickle. She twirls into Ditch's legs, falls, spreads over him.

"Whoops."

Ditch puts a hand on her soft damp back.

"Do you like it?" Suzie asks, bringing her face up to his. "It's velour."

She leads the way to the bed, giggling, refusing to turn on any lights. In the bedroom a pale street lamp catches her through the window. Ditch looks at her breasts, touches them, thinks of her face in frames of cold light, the permeable darkness.

She pushes him away.

"Take your pants off."

He pulls out of his wet jeans.

Later, walking back, he remembers it. He thinks that it wasn't what he expected. Not the thing itself, exactly, but the why of it, the how of it. Stopping suddenly, he checks his pockets, feels like he left something there, feels like he's late for an appointment he never made. Cancel, postpone, reschedule, call in sick. A loss more tangible than any act of truancy. He doesn't know where he's supposed to be. In front of his own door, he stops just short of ringing the bell, like a stranger would. What's she doing up there? he thinks. And: *I'll never be home again.*

Barbara hears footsteps above her. She holds her breath, stays very still.

The wind bucks, rivets of air sloping against the shingles, throwing branches from the fat old oak in the front yard onto the roof. She gropes at the sound, hoping that the clattering will yield to the gentle pad of footsteps.

She hears a scrape, like the door closing. She waits, used air stuck in her throat. It could have been anything: pitching wind, fat rain drops. She breathes again, and the sound fills her ears. The upstairs apartment occupied by a keening silence.

2

Debs wasn't exactly a runaway like she thought she'd be.

She just wakes up and finds herself alone in the house with no one there, and no one there, and later, no one there.

It's ten minutes after the hour. At the university, classes are just starting. Ditch cuts the engine. Silence. Beside the van a field of soft grass, trees dropping leaves. It's not too late, he thinks. I could still go back. Study hard, get good grades. But thinking it makes it seem so unlikely — thinking about anything sticks it in the past.

Ditch opens his door.

"All right," he says.

He grabs four bundles of newspapers from the back. One under each arm, and one in each hand. Plastic cord cuts into his skin. He takes the wide concrete stairs two at a time. His body hunches forward under the weight.

It gets warmer, then colder. One night it snows again. The traffic snakes through the side streets, white flakes sucked into headlights, slush cresting wheel wakes. In the morning, Debs turns on the clock radio the guy downstairs gave her. A present. The people are nice here in Canada. If this was home, the announcer would be in a panic, barely able to keep up with all the schools and offices closing as a result of the deep freeze. She is on the floor of a strange room wrapped in the blanket he lent her, the landlady's son.

The announcer talks.

Debs tucks the blanket under her, so the cold air won't seep in. She closes her eyes. She imagines the thick white snow, hugs her body, thinking — Daddy. What would you give to be with me right now?

He doesn't answer. There are only disc jockey jokes about plunging temperatures, dangerous wind chills, a cold front sweeping over from someplace called Winnipeg. Debs thinks of thick sweaters, parkas, fur-lined hats, sheepskin gloves. For the first time in her life she can itemize her possessions, her inadequate clothing: a pair of sweatpants. A silk dress. Two t-shirts. A sweatshirt. Underwear.

She sits up. The bundled blanket falls around her waist. No school cancellations, no meetings rescheduled, no epic traffic jams. Just the unfamiliar white stuff drifting from the sky and landing on the blotchy shells of dirty cars. Her skin in the morning air. She can do whatever she wants.

I've got to get a sweater or something — is it always so cold?

Ditch opens the door. He was going to call out to her. Say something —

She could be asleep or in the bathroom or maybe she's sick —
Some kind of flu going around.

He doesn't say anything.

He moves to the window. A green sheet pinned up. If she comes home, he thinks, I won't even see her.

On the wood floor, a quilt. He crouches beside it, smoothing a corner down. The legs in his muscles, strained, blurred. He picks a long hair off. Where she sleeps. Against the wall there's the laptop, plugged in, turned on. Ditch stares at it. The neat little keyboard, letters lined up against each other, the bright screen shimmering green blue.

A husk, empty inside.

There is also the bare bedroom, blank space, telephone line plugged into the wall, cord trailing out.

He moves into the kitchen. The bare counter, gleaming.

He turns away, opens the refrigerator. Also empty. What does she eat?

He returns to the living room, stands over the tiny computer, listens for steps on the stairs. He's waiting for her. They were supposed to spend the day together. He asked her — a date. No — something else —

He crouches, runs his finger over a cool plastic surface. Shifts in his pants. His sudden hard-on.

Morts has testicular cancer.

Cancer of the balls, he tells people.

He imagines the girl under her heap of oversized sweaters. He feels something. Not exactly lust. The pain though.

"Hi," the girl says. "I want a job."

Morts fingers his moustache. Before the cancer he was wet, pale and pudgy, his hands shook when he poured shots.

The girl pulls her hat off. Thin rays of light spill over her shoulders.

"I can work," she says. She looks around. "I can work here."

How long will it take? This dying? The doctors — what do they know? He had stood up in the waiting room to walk out. The receptionist appeared as he opened the door and called his name.

At least she knew my name.

Morts takes two glasses and pours them each a shot. His hands are steady and his forehead is dry like old bone.

"It's a bit early," he says, shrugging. "But, you know…"

He knocks his back. "I'm dying," he says.

Debs sips.

"I'm sorry."

"Don't be."

Debs shrugs like a pirouette.

"I don't know. I've already got a girl. Comes in nights."

Debs shrugs again. Looks around. Almost laughs. "Maybe you need two?"

The way her eyes go right through him.

The bar is empty. Mostly empty.
The phone rings and Debs answers it.
"Hello?"
"Hello?"
A man breathing.
"Is, uh, would your mother be —"
"She's dead. Do you want to talk to my dad?"
[click]

That night, she's afraid to go back to the apartment. She's afraid of her daddy's grey box, inert lump of circuits and wires, magic carpet ride to another world, to a threat, to a promise.

She goes back anyway.

Everything is black.

— but the site is still here. At least it's still here —

Debs stares at the screen. Not empty, not shut down by its anonymous server, just closed into itself — asleep, she thinks. She stares until she sees a faint pulse, tears welling up, dripping.

It could have been a diary, a journal, an electronic scribble pad of random thoughts, an account file to keep track of her tips, expenses, what comes in, what goes out. Ditch has some cash saved up. He doesn't pay rent and his mom buys the groceries. He offers to chip in but she never lets him, keeps saying he should be "saving for the future." What future? Debs's mother is dead. Murdered. He imagines her beautiful, full of awful beauty. He spits in the sink, runs the tap, sips water from his palm. He swallows.

Down the stairs much later. Sliding out of the apartment, locking the door. Thinking: it's empty, there's no one here.

He waited for her.

A house slowly settling into the open earth.

I'm living in Toronto now. That's in Canada. Ever been? I want you to know that whatever happened, I forgive you. Things won't always be this way.

When you find me, Daddy, don't be mad at me. No matter what. I check the website every morning as soon as I get home from the bar, around 4 a.m., the sun isn't up yet, the air goes all gray from black, but it's fall here almost winter and it's cold and it's dark most of the time, it seems, it's dark but I'm not tired when I get home. I'm too excited, I can't wait to get home and be with you, we always do a few shots while we're closing up, and I think of you, I'm a drinker now too Daddy.

◫ I wonder if you'd like Morts. I catch him looking at me and he blushes. The way he looks at me, though, like he wants to hollow me out and put himself inside. That's how I know he's dying for real. He jokes about it with Suzie and everyone else but never with me. Did you kill her? I don't have any furniture. The floor is hard. Morts says everyone is dangerous, everyone is scum, don't trust anyone. He looks at me. I live in the second-floor apartment of a house. It's a big apartment. I got it cheap. There are two people who live below me in the downstairs apartment. They own the house. The mother hates me because the son likes me. I don't know why the mother hates me. Her son comes to the bar and drinks. Suzie says she slept with him. How could you have lived with her all those years? The other night an old drunk grabbed me from behind, cupped my tits with his filthy hands. I dropped a tray of glasses. Everyone was looking. I'm not a virgin. The guy said fucking bitch. He was going to try and strangle me, but Morts whacked him with the baseball bat he keeps behind the bar. He's sentimental or something. Morts is strong, because he's dying. The boy from downstairs was there. He came up to me after and asked me if I was okay, said if I wanted he would wait for me to walk me home. I laughed and drank the shot of dark rum Morts gave me to steady my nerves. I was up all morning and afternoon after I got home. Staring at the computer screen, thinking how it felt, his hands on me, the sound of Morts hitting him with the baseball bat. It sounded like someone dropping a big rock into water. The screen was gray, not black. Where are you Daddy? Are you there? When I got to the bar the next night Suzie gave me two pills to help me stay awake. I took them with a shot of rye. I drink rye, it tastes like your breath. I stay awake with pills. I'm afraid I might miss something.

Today I saw it. I don't know what it was but I saw it. You sent it to me. For hours afterwards I didn't move, I didn't even blink. A faint outline, a box, a picture, something. I felt so good, knowing you were telling me something. Finally! I don't know what it is yet but I will. What is it? There was a stabbing pain and I looked down and saw that my big toe was bleeding. The skin around the nail, I guess I picked it off, I didn't know what I was doing. I'm sorry. It was an accident. I don't know how it happened. When I looked up, the screen was black again. But it was there, what-ever it was. I did see it. One time the police came to the door. Watch out. They were looking for you.

🖂 Sometimes I think I can be happy. I really do.

What's the first word I ever said? I didn't take any pictures with me when I left, but I wish I had, the one of you and me when I was eight and you were wearing that ugly Hawaiian shirt. She hated it. She gave it to her boyfriend at the meat-packing plant when you were out of town. I saw her give it to him. Had the day off yesterday. I let Ditch come up for a bit, he said he'd show me more of the city when it got warm. He says in the summer Toronto gets hot. I acted all surprised. He's sweet. I told him I was sleepy, that he had to go. He didn't try and kiss me or anything. Did you go on dates with her? At first, I mean.

After work I got high with Suzie and Morts. It was my first time getting high. I felt warm and very happy. Then Morts pulled out a bottle of what he always says is the good stuff though I can't tell the difference like you probably can. It was snowing outside, it does that a lot here. It makes me think of Mr. Leblanc, our next-door neighbor, and how funny he was. I started laughing and they said — What? What's so funny? But I didn't tell them. How could I tell them? I just said that there was this guy — a French-Canadian diplomat who used to — and then everyone started laughing. Morts patted the top of my head and poured us another shot. Then Morts says that if he was as beautiful as me he would be right now in Tahiti lying in the sun and drinking iced fruit drinks and rum, just lying there and letting someone else take care of him. Suzie put her arm around him and nobody said anything. After a while Morts laughed and drank straight out of the bottle. He passed the bottle to me and I drank and started to laugh too, and I spilled some whiskey down my shirt.

Daddy there's blood. I looked at it in the bathroom and I threw up. It smells so bad, it smells yellow. I just woke up and it was like that. I threw up, then, all over myself. It hurts that much. It hurts to even look at it. I don't know what happened. I don't know what to do. I tried to wash my foot under warm water but when the water hit my toe I think I fainted. I was already in the tub, so I didn't make much noise or bang my head or anything. I don't know how it happened. I get out of the tub and find the camera I bought from the drugstore the other day. I take pictures of myself, naked, spread out in the tub. I use all the film, I take the same picture over and over again. I'm alone, Daddy, I swear. I'm alone. When I woke up my skin was cold. I held my hand up to my face and I could see right through it, I could see everything. I was so afraid. I was shaking. My foot was down there a long way away. I couldn't feel it any more. The nail was gone and there was a shell of blood and the tip of the toe was turning purple and a bit orange. I couldn't feel anything but the smell was terrible. Daddy, look for me on my website, I've put the pictures up, all the same picture. I took the picture myself, it's me there. In the tub. I'm sorry, I couldn't think of any other way. Will you recognize me? When was the last time you saw me naked? I can't get up. I'm just concentrating on you and the two meeting lines you sent, your message to me. It's too cold, anyone can see that, but I can't get up. I don't know what it means.

www.debstub.com

There is a TV in the corner over the bar. The sound is turned off and instead there are words written on the screen. It's supposed to be for the deaf. Morts always keeps the TV on the channel with shows about medicine. The Health Network. It's like he's obsessed or something. Every night there is an hour of operations. Morts watches. Won't pour drinks or talk while the show is on. One night when it was really late they were showing something old in black and white. It was a man making a long-distance call from an office in Canada to his mother in Scotland. It was Christmas. Before he was going to make the call, they showed him walking around the snowy streets looking in windows, watching children line up to talk to Santa Claus. Then he is talking on the phone. He holds the receiver tight, pushes it into his face like he can't hear. He nods fast. He isn't talking, someone else is talking. His lips are pressed together. Someone else is talking and we don't know what they are saying. His mother is talking. His lips finally move, gently, slowly. I don't know how you know it's his mother who's talking. You just know. *I wish I was too*, it says on the screen under him. The words are yellow. The camera is just on his face, his hand holding the phone. You can see that he is crying. *Mother* in yellow. *Goodbye, Mother* in yellow.

✉ Your baby girl. I took those pictures myself. I was alone. It's true, I swear. My bad foot hooked over the edge of the tub, dripping. Daddy, I've put it up on the web for you. I get 18,000 hits a day. It's just the same pictures over and over again. But they love me, they come back to look at me every day. They send me e-mails, beg me to marry them, to put up a picture of me doing myself with a dildo, or drinking cum out of a test tube. I did it so you could find me. But now I don't know. There's a boy. He lives downstairs.

I met Suzie in front of the bar. I was supposed to meet Ditch, but Suzie said she didn't want to. They slept together once, but she won't tell me about it. I felt bad about not hooking up with him like I said I was going to. He waited all day, I'm sure. We took the streetcar. I had never been on the streetcar before. I didn't have any change. Everyone was looking at me. Suzie laughed. Everyone looking. I laughed too. We went shopping and Suzie tried everything on. The women who worked at the stores didn't think we would buy anything. I kept smiling. We didn't buy anything. Then we went for coffee. We drank about 18 cups. Suzie asked me about Ditch, about why I invited him. She says she thinks he's cute but he's weird. I said that I didn't know, that I just invited him. She looked at me and shrugged. You're weird too, she said. She's older than me but pretends she isn't. She has freckles on her nose. We walked over to a bar. We held hands. Suzie uses some kind of mousse in her hair. I've never had a martini before. Suzie rolls her eyes when I tell her. We get up to go to another bar. I'm dizzy. Suzie holds on to me. She says that I should eat something, that I never eat. We go to another bar and she tells me about some guy she had sex with from Buffalo who wanted her to move there with him. She still talks to him. She says she doesn't want a boyfriend ever. Now he's mostly her drug connection. I tell her my first was Bobby. I fucked him in the basement. You were away on business. Everyone was away. He said my nipples were sweet, like ripe cherries. Suzie thought that was hilarious. Ripe cherries. We laughed. We ordered two shots of something because Suzie said we had to celebrate. It was thick and tasted like licorice.

Ditch puts his napkin on his lap. It slides off. Excuse me, he says. He bends down, grabs it. They're eating dinner together. Debs look at him, amused, not quite smiling. The inseparable quiet. The sound of cutlery resting up against half-full plates. The jingle of ice inside glass. Murmuring voices inside his head:

What is it like to know you are dying? What is it like to not remember anything? What is it like to be from nowhere?

"I waited for you," he says. "I waited."

Debs says: "Once I forgot my sweater in the car. That was ten years ago. My mother slapped me."

Ditch looks over at her.

"What about your father?"

She tells him about the time she forgot her sweater in the car and they had already walked a block on the way to see her mother's meat-packing boyfriend and she had said she was cold, she had said: I'm cold, Mommy. I'm cold.

"What about your father?" he says again.

Debs picks up a fork. Puts the fork down again.

It's hot in the restaurant.

Debs holds on to the arms of her chair. She tells Ditch she hopes he understands. It's winter. It's almost winter. A taste in his mouth.

He thinks of his mother, watching TV alone in her bedroom.

Debs touches his hand. "Do you understand?" she says.

"Sure. Sure I do."

Closing the door and stepping out into the hallway and hearing the television laughter and then opening the front door and closing it and locking it and walking quickly down the sidewalk, on his way to meet Debs at the restaurant.

Debs takes her hand away.

"I want to understand," he says quickly. "I do."

She touches him, grazes his palm with a single finger.

"I'm sorry," he says. "I just — when I was waiting for you — I thought, I was worried that you — so I went into Knudtsen's — your — the apartment. There's no food in the fridge. On the floor, that little computer."

Debs laughs.

"It's nothing," she says. "Just stories."

"I didn't mean to —"

She stirs her coffee, hitting the spoon against the side of the cup. She pulls her spoon out, coffee dripping on a white saucer. Drops it on the table.

"I'm sorry," Ditch says.

Debs stands up, drops a bill on the table.

"No, c'mon, let me —" He fumbles for his wallet.

"Forget it," Debs says. "It's not important. Your funny coloured money."

She wraps a thrift-store threadbare cardigan around her like she might disappear.

Outside the restaurant the air getting colder. Debs squeezes his arm. She stops on the sidewalk, pulls him against her. She kisses his cheek.

He says: "Next time let me pay. I mean, isn't the guy supposed to pay?"

She laughs into his ear. Fall sweeps against them.

Ditch unlocks the door. Steps in. He moves slowly, as if carrying something he's already dropped. He looks back at her. Debs pulls him into her. She giggles, tosses her hair.

"I've been thinking," she says. "You saw mine, now I want to see yours."

Ditch struggles to smile.

"Your apartment," Debs says.

"You want to see my apartment?"

"It's only fair."

Ditch feels his legs, his hand in his pocket curling around his keys. In the tiny foyer, the authoritarian whisper of the late-night news. The smell of the returning cold on their clothes, in their hair.

Debs pokes him, laughing.

"Hey," Ditch says, pulling away.

"Hay is for horses." She digs into his pocket. Their fingers wrestling. Her warm hand in his loose jeans. Laughing, they fall against each other. The door swings open.

"Mom, uh, hi." Ditch tries to step away from Debs but she presses against him, her fingers in his pocket against his thigh.

Barbara clears her throat, pulls her robe tight.

"Hi," Debs says, raising her free hand.

"You coming in?" Barbara says, looking at Ditch.

Ditch leads the way past his mother, Debs trailing, dragging her hand slowly out of his pocket.

Barbara closes the door behind them, turns the lock. The bolt whispers shut.

"The kitchen," Ditch points out. "A little bigger than what you have upstairs, but basically the same."

"Sit down," Barbara says, appearing behind them. "Sit down. I'll fix you a snack. How about a chicken sandwich? The way I make it, Ditch's favourite. Sit down. You're both so skinny."

"No, Mom, it's okay."

"Sit down."

Ditch looks at Debs. She shrugs and slumps into one of the wooden kitchen chairs. She smiles at them, mother and son, each wearing the same expression: exasperation, bewilderment, fear.

Barbara puts food on the table: cheese, crackers, a bowl of grapes.

"Thank you," Debs says. "You don't have to go to all this trouble." She smiles, Ditch watches the corners of her face bunch together in perfect marbles.

"Mom," he says, "it's okay."

"Would anyone like tea?"

Debs pops a grape in her mouth, stifles a yawn, works a piece of cheese around her fingers.

"Well," she says. "I didn't realize it was so late." She stands up, moves behind Ditch, ruffles his hair. His cheeks flush. "Ditch, walk me to the door?" She throws the cheese bit in her mouth. "Good night," she says to Barbara. "Thanks for the snack."

Out the door, halfway into the gloom. He's limp in her arms. Her lips hard against his.

Ditch cracks the window. The sound of wind rushing against the van. The cold air flows in. He shivers. Rolls up the window. He's thinking about the bar, about going there. He shrugs. He sits up straight. She's avoiding me, since last week.

He doesn't blame her.

He shouldn't have — her computer — when do things start to feel real? Now? Ever? No, he definitely shouldn't have.

"Wake up, big boy. Gotta wake up now."

In the donut shop Ditch fidgets. Good Time Donuts and Deli. Or is it Good Times? He doesn't much like the donut shop.

"How's the traffic out there?" Carla asks. She plops down in the seat next to him, sighs, lights a cigarette. It's late, lunch rush over. Just Ditch and the regulars on break from the supermarket across the street. The regulars. I keep coming here. I don't have to. Carla makes a big show of stretching, arching her back. Ditch looks out the window.

Five days a week. Time is the route, a game he keeps playing though it's the same every time. They aren't friends. He doesn't have any friends. He looks at the half sandwich in his hands. The usual. It's Friday. He chews mechanically, swallows, puts the sandwich down on a chipped plate.

"Hey, you look different." Carla blows grey smoke. "You got yourself a new pal?"

His legs are dull, as if his body understands what's going to happen but his mind has no idea. He covers his face with a copy of today's edition, pretends to scan the headlines.

"A girl?" Carla persists.

The way she hurried up the stairs. The way the door closed. Her body. Up the stairs like a ghost. Barbara behind him, shaking her head, disgusted. Debs closed the door. The gentle click. He thought, then, that he had already seen everything — not everything — her computer, the anonymous calibration of words — *do you understand?*

Carla purses meaningful smoke.

"Bye, guys," she says as the meat department lurches by. The head butcher waves, a fat grin on his face like a snout. Carla laughs, winks Ditch in the ribs. *Well?*

The van smells of wet rotting newspaper, a fleshy, decomposing reek. Ditch drives, half dreams. He's stuck in quicksand, pulling at Knudtsen's loose body. He shakes his head, cracks the window. Cold grey air harbours its own essence: another weathered morning, his face set, the big tires turning over themselves. Ditch complaining into the wind: "I hate this, it stinks in here. It really stinks."

He swerves into the fast lane, accelerates, shoots by a cop car.

Spinning his wrist, he furiously cranks the window down. Picks a spot on the dashboard and keeps his gaze on it. Won't look up. Feels his eyes water.

"He's dead," Ditch says.

The next day or the day after:

The van makes its way up a stately side street. Cars in a slow processional.

"Pick up the pace," Ditch mutters. "Give it some gas."

"If they want to kill me," Morts says to Debs, "they should just kill me." He holds her gaze for a moment. She's the one who doesn't look away.

Debs fills his glass with whiskey, takes a quick swallow herself, puts a hand on his shoulder. He has regrets. A child he doesn't remember. A woman who loved him the way he could never love anything. She squeezes lightly, rushes off with a tray of drinks.

Soon, he thinks she might have said.

Morts wakes up. The bar is packed. It's all he can do to raise his head and look around. Kids. Morts hears them talking in the distance. The future. They laugh and lean into each other, bodies against bodies.

He sleeps and Debs passes in the night like a daydream, refilling his glass, wiping his face with a damp cloth, gently pressing her lips against the crown of his balding head.

The first thing Ditch sees is Morts. Morts propped up in one of those tall wooden bar chairs. His eyes are closed and his mouth hangs open, an obelisk leading into darkness. Ditch imagines the peppery sheen of black stubble on his face. Tiny hairs sprouting through the pallid expanse, each miniature crevice dotted by some meticulous pointillist.

Ditch stands on the bottom step. He looks for Debs, squints through the glass of the door. He doesn't want to go in — an admission, inevitable, he needs her now — he doesn't want to need her.

He sees Morts again through the smoke haze, the curves of flashing faces, the glass blurred with years of grime. The room of golden glowing people. Above Morts, above his lolling head, an operation proceeds. Green-gowned figures hunch over a prone body. The camera moves in: white glove hands flexing. The beat of an exposed organ — If he dies, Ditch thinks, they'll shave him. It grows back, but they'll shave him.

There's a long lineup for drinks. People stand at the bar smoking furiously and waving handfuls of ten- and twenty-dollar bills. *Your funny coloured money.* No one seems to notice Morts in the corner. When did it get so — it used to be...empty —

"Hiya, Ditch," Suzie says. She puts her arms around his neck, hugs him. "Where ya been?" Her breasts against his chest. He shrugs. She lets go of him, steps back. "So, you and Debs, you and her — I guess you don't need me any more, huh? Oh well. Lucky boy." She giggles. "Look at this crowd. I've got to get back to the bar. All of a sudden — we're a hit — it's crazy." Suzie shrugs. "Don't ask me why. Stranger things have happened. I guess." She laughs again, acting it out, playing a role. Ditch can't think of anything to say. "Well," Suzie goes, "I gotta get back to work. Hey — guess who's here. Bobby. Remember Bobby?"

Suzie grabs Ditch, pulls him over to Bobby's table. She leans forward and whispers something in Bobby's ear. He laughs, nods. His head flapping against asphalt. Suzie saunters through the crowd, butter on toast.

"What an ass she has," Bobby says. "And I think she still likes ya." Bobby jabs at Ditch's belly with a short fat finger. "Don't ask me why."

"Shut up," Ditch mutters. Bobby's head cracking pavement. Shouting 1-2-3. Suzie shrieking, laughing, the same sound, no sound, nothing at all.

"Ah, but you've got the porn queen." Bobby points at Debs, fixing drinks behind the bar. "That must be something."

Ditch stares at Morts, propped up on his chair under the television. Blood splatters over a shiny scalpel. Ditch stands up. His chair falls back.

"Hey, where ya going?" Bobby leers.

"What are you talking about?" Ditch says.

"What, you don't know? Everyone knows. What do you think we're all doing in this dump? The porn queen, here, your girlfriend. She's got a website up. I've seen it. Her pics are everywhere. She's, like, in the tub. Naked." Bobby giggles at the word: *Naked.*

"She's not my girlfriend."

"Hey, whatever man. You don't believe me. She's the main attraction. There's just one thing I don't get. So do me a favour, man, check out her feet. Next time you two are, ya know..."

Ditch swings the beer bottle. He hears a sound: the satisfying shatter of a grin; and under that, the agreeable silence, the bar's hushed complicity — in this, in everything.

"Why'd you do it?"

"He insulted you."

"What did he say?" Her smile. The white under it.

Ditch staggers against her. He's drunk. He's been drinking.

"I missed you," Debs says. She lowers her head, looks down at the sidewalk. "They had to call an ambulance. The police..."

The wind, darkness into darkness.

"You didn't miss me," he says. He kicks at the pavement with his boot. "I want you to show me how to work it," he says feverishly. "That tiny computer. Show me what it does, what's so important?"

She leans into him. Her smooth hand slides into the grip of his fingers.

"It's getting cold," Ditch says.

"It doesn't matter," Debs says.

Suzie watches through the window.

"They're kissing," she says. "I should call the cops." Morts is asleep. His uneven breathing, a line of wet saliva catching on his stubbly chin. Suzie drinks from a bottle of thick green liquid. "They're both crazy."

The steps creak. The door hushes shut and Debs drapes over him. Darkness, a faint emerald pulse, the street light through the sheet hung over the window. *My mother doesn't wait up for me, she used to —*

Even the light in the foyer — switched off. Debs cold, her thin lips icy against his cheek. Suddenly, Ditch is reluctant, feels her peck wet and swampy like a quicksand kiss on the lips. He needs it to be perfect. Not like with Suzie —

"Ditch," she says, breaking away from him. "You ever feel like you're, I dunno, going, insane?" She laughs, pressing against herself. "I mean, do you ever see something and think that you really can't be seeing what you're seeing?"

He should offer up some rapturous affirmation: Don't worry, I'll love you forever, I'll die with your secret, *you can tell me, baby.*

But it all seems so inevitable, familiar. He doesn't know what she's talking about. He knows what she's talking about. Debs moves through the gloom to the far wall. She opens the laptop. A blue triangle. A crackling noise fills the blank room then drains off. Ditch moves toward the spilled beacon of light. He crouches next to her. Her perfect face, pearl framed in blonde hair, grey marble eyes reflecting the halo glow of the computer screen. Ditch blinks, shifts forward. He has this sudden feeling of motion, like he's driving. On the screen he can see a big house, a verdant front lawn. He looks at the computer, then back at Debs. He's not the one going crazy. He told her he understood, he wants her to know that he understands. And in a way he does. His legs ache under him. This is it? he thinks. What is this?

✉ I slip into Daddy's study and turn on his computer. I see what he sees: naked girls doing what they do, sucking (or else: me chewing on the bottom of a pen waiting for scrolling — face, tits, belly, pussy).

I can go into his study and lock the door and look all I want and no one would ever have a thing to say about it. My back pressed hard into the cool leather of his chair. His website.

WWW.CRABGIRLS.COM

All uppercase. That's my Daddy. I squirm. A woman on all fours pushing against the cock in her ass.

The Parent screaming —

Where the hell are you? Bitch.

This is what my father likes.

When Debs wakes up they are banging on the door.

"Open up. Police. Open up. We know you're in there."

She peers into the world, her eyes tiny cracks in her face. She stretches, the coarse fronds of the short carpet rubbing against her lower back. At least she isn't in her bed, curled in terror under the down comforter, the light streaming through the fuchsia blinds making everything blood-pink.

She pulls her knees to her chest. It isn't brave what she's doing. Locking herself in Daddy's study, falling asleep on the rug. Now it's morning, she tells herself. And everything will be all right. They've found them. They're dead. Of course, how else would they be? She pictures them, two corpses lying naked on crushed black velvet, their bodies soft and white. The Parent never tans. She hates the sun. The Parent —

A fist against the front door. Debs slowly makes her way down the stairs. They can search the place, ask her anything.

She has already erased the last message, inscribing its contents in her mind.

She stops at the bottom of the stairs, shivers. Bare feet disappearing on white carpet. The knocking. The shouts turning to voices. She smells smoke and thinks, suddenly, that behind the door is her father, eyes glazed over, lips pursed around a broken cigarette.

She pushes the breath out of her body, draws the deadbolt, puts her hand on the gold knob.

"Who's in there?"

"Open the door."

"Now."

She imagines: two young men, hands on their guns, handcuffs dangling from their belts, blue caps cocked over wide shiny foreheads.

Her hand drops from the doorknob. She takes a step back. Her fingers waver. The door flies open. She falls, blinded by a sudden gash of morning.

They pull her up.

"Are you okay?" They are rumpled in cheap tan sports jackets, the worried one plump and ample but, like his leaner, taller partner, not particularly young or good-looking. The other one keeps his distance. He wears gloves.

Ditch imagines living there. It isn't a mansion. Four, maybe five bedrooms, living room, dining room, study, den, three bathrooms, one kitchen. (Plus a kitchenette in the basement.) Nothing huge. Just what's necessary to be comfortable, to keep up, to live well, to live life the way one becomes accustomed to living life.

A house, shuttered windows in rows, red bricks, bushes growing against the front under the big bay window of the piano room. Nothing extravagant or exceptional. A Japanese cherry tree off to the side of the driveway. True, the shrubs look a little ragged, the tulips are crowded, the grass is longer than you might expect. A glamorous sunflower askew, bent over double.

Ditch stares. He stares at the scene, imagining it as real. He leans closer into the recognizable quotient of it, the sheer fact of it being not a picture, but exactly what a picture could never be. The blades of grass tremble. The bushes are dark and thick. The tree's absent shadow — it's night, Ditch thinks dully, it's dark. The darkness is the only real aberration. Otherwise it's all so totally normal.

"My father's in there," Debs whispers.

He turns to look at her. He falls out of his crouch onto his knees. Her face is blank. Her face soaking in the blue glow, pressed into the screen, so close her nose is almost touching it. He reaches out to feel her shoulder. She slips against him.

Her face twists in some distant ecstasy. Her fingers claw into his back as he fumbles. Open to him, her eyes turn away like an ocean reflection.

Afterwards she doesn't speak. She stands up, keeps her legs pressed together to hold his sperm inside.

He follows her into the bathroom. She stops in front of the tub. He turns on the taps, adjusts them to the right temperature, plugs the drain. When the bath is ready, she steps in. She sits down in the tub, spreads her legs. Ditch tries to see her posed on the computer screen, splayed out in the tub, her face flushed from the heat of the water or some other exertion, her body loose and glowing, called up from nowhere by the hissing screech of the modem, pulled out of nothing — but for what? This distant rite, a furry crackle of ritual, that ghostly blue and then all this, all of this in front of him, in front of everybody.

She leans forward and he washes her back. The white soap disappears against her skin. He rubs the froth in, his fingers gliding against the split between her buttocks. She sits in the bath. She is his picture, his evidence that something happened. He remembers this feeling; something happened — What happened?

She falls back against the slope of the tub. He trails soap between her breasts, lathers a light ruffle of hair. His penis pressed against the cold side of the tub as he crouches forward to wash her chest, her soft, slightly protruding belly. She pulls at him and he follows her pull, slipping into the tub, crouching between her legs. Her fingers move. She strokes and he runs his palms over. Her fist closes like an explanation. Questions he should have asked her. He shuts his eyes, tries to think about Suzie, that first time, breath in puffs of aged smoke, newspaper grey spreading over flesh disappearing into flesh.

But instead he remembers his father holding him in the air, tossing him up, catching him while he laughs, his mouth in a frightened baby oval, open. Or is that just a picture in his mother's album? — an image fossilized in his mind. Her hand faster now, he arches his body to meet the touch. Will he forget this too? His life, nothing more than a storage bank for obsolete memories. A photograph. A video. A diary entry. Old newspapers spewing out the back, burying everything.

Debs starts talking, snapping him out of his reverie. Her voice is quiet and monotone, like someone flipped a switch. Her fingers, meanwhile, slow, working.

"It started as nothing. Grey light. I stared at it. I checked it every day, because I knew there would be something, there had to be, he sent me an e-mail telling me to look there, at this spot, at this site. So I knew. But at first there was nothing and I would run home from the bar and just stare for hours. It got so I could sit straight through the morning and afternoon until it was time to go back to the bar. All day. It's like something you look at far in the distance. If you don't keep your eyes on it, it will just disappear. That's the way he did things, like they were about to disappear. I couldn't stand being away from the screen. I waited. I waited everywhere. Here. At the bar. The lines started to look like the edges of a house, a building. I cried when I saw what it was. There were moments when I could see a lawn, even people. Not their faces. But then everything would go grey again and I would wait all morning, all afternoon for the image to clear up and sometimes it wouldn't."

Ditch pulses to her rhythm, his skin charged, she's talking about the house, he thinks, the picture of the house she showed me. Only he realizes, now, that it wasn't a picture. It was real, it was what was really happening. But it all seems so — the way she touches him — he won't ask questions. Just brings himself forward to meet the tide of her, crashing over him.

"He wanted me to get away. But I can't. He can't. It's too late for that. They say he killed my mother, but I know he didn't. He didn't kill anyone. Once I saw him in there, not him, a shape, a face, I knew it was him just from the shadow. Then everything went dark. It was night. I couldn't see into the windows. And I knew he was in there, had to be. The police showed up. Those detectives. The ones who kept asking me all those horrible questions. They think they know. They think he's guilty. They like it like this, a fugitive making his last stand, it's better this way, they tell each other, no trial, no evidence. Blood on the walls of my bedroom. They'll go in there and shoot him, because they can, because they think no one knows what's happening, what's happened. They think they know all about it, but what do they know? Why did he go back there? Why did he send me the message? He's killing himself. Is that what he wants me to see? That she's driven him to it, in the end, after all, despite everything, fucking bitch, it's her, she's the one making him do this. I think they're going to kill him. That's what this is all about. Watching him die. It's like he's killing himself. For me. Because of her. To save me from her. But it's impossible. I don't need his fucking help. Where the fuck was he when I needed his help? And now he's taking the blame. Acting crazy. He's got some kind of camera up in the trees. It's live, it's really happening."

Debs's voice picks up speed. Her small fist sliding just a little faster. But it's even, never excited, never hysterical, never random. It's Ditch who thrusts and grunts and splashes water out of the tub, the words raining on him, but he's already wet, he doesn't notice, he pumps forward, a little faster. My first hand job, he thinks.

"They're going to kill him, of course they are, that's what they're going to do. You saw them. The fat one, the skinny one, they came after me too. But I got away. He helped me get away. Sometimes the screen goes grey again. I'm afraid it's over, it's too late, they've done — or he's — they think they know what he's done, they think they have the one they want. I have to go back. You have to take me back. I can't go alone. They're saying — they think he's a murderer. But they're wrong. There are things I can't tell anyone. Things I didn't mean to do. I have to go back."

Ditch grunts, thrusts forward in her wet hands.

She opens her eyes, surprised.

"You," she says.

She sleeps. He cleans and bandages her feet. Strips of skin peeled off in meticulous layers. Hours of labour, the fruit of the flesh laid bare. He shakes when he touches her. The sun comes up, morning. They could have been anywhere, and he wishes they were, anywhere, somewhere, a place they'd never been, a place with a history.

He covers her with a blanket, tucks it under her slatted ribs. Her head next to the small computer. She thinks he understands. It's all just stories to him. Like seeing things you can't possibly be seeing. Like saying things you never meant for yourself to say:

Have you ever gone —?

He's never been anywhere.

He hears the door shut downstairs. He runs to the window, slips in front of the green sheet into the blind light of morning. My mother. If she turns around, she'll see me. He wants her to turn around.

He leaves the window. Pulls into his jeans. The crust of yesterday's socks gives as he shoves his feet into his boots. He touches a finger to his lips, places it on her forehead. He turns away and slinks out of the apartment. Downstairs, he holds the front door so it won't crash shut. He forces his legs into a march, long strides in the direction he saw his mother take. He catches sight of her: some blocks up, a receding figure.

Her arms swing.

He is conscious of his own body, so unwilling, so out of control. What happened keeps happening — Bobby — he couldn't, he didn't mean to — but then, it wasn't quite — an accident. His legs are loose, flapping. All the energy gone, not gone, transferred, as if to a different department. He follows her, the consuming space between the city blocks. In his mind he turns behind him and sees nothing but a vast emptiness, the distance between what he wants and what he gets. I fucked her. And, already, he doesn't remember. Is she crazy? *The police — Bobby — I shouldn't have —*

Barbara pauses at the corner. He stops, presses against a doorway. He's too close — She'll see me. It's cold. He steps gingerly around the building's edge, half expecting her to appear grim-faced in front of him, shaking her head, disgust, disappointment, spying on her, his mother who loves him. What is he capable of? These hands. These legs. He's hard again, thinking about Debs; what he did with her, what they've done.

He follows Barbara, a trim figure in a long pea-green coat. She moves slowly under the arched entryway. He puts his hands in his pockets to adjust the crotch of his jeans. Where is she? He sees it now, recognizes it, a few limousines, a gaggle of teary-eyed mourners, say goodbye, he thinks, say goodbye. She loved him. Didn't she? He moves past the cemetery gates, flung open. An invitation.

He finds her at the grave. Watches through the angled gaps of tombstones. The sun behind her, shining in his eyes. He squints, sees her breath in sheets of white. He takes a step back, the air comes at him, the grass bends under his boots, hard frost on the blades. It's cold. He's cold and stupid in dirty jeans and the good sweater, not his delivery sweater, not the sweater he wears in his dreams, the soft swish of frayed fabric as he works feverishly to bury what he doesn't know. He has two sweaters. Barbara stands in front of Knudtsen's stone. She doesn't talk or cry. He doesn't think she's crying. I'm spying on my mother — she shifts from foot to foot, her collar pulled up, her face tired, vulnerable. He urges his legs around the markers, stepping over buried bodies.

"Ditch, what are you — Ditch. Oh, Ditch. Look at you."

She holds on to him, a small woman clinging to her son.

"You aren't even wearing a coat," she says.

He tries to swallow. The weight in his throat. He wants to ask her about his father. If she thinks it matters, if he mattered. Would his presence have changed everything? Anything? A little boy tossed in the air. His arms wrapped around her. The urge to comb his hair and tweak his collar and advise him on the proper time at which a thank-you note should be sent, these things he wants so much to escape from, the reason he holds her. The cold air alive around them. The city's dead slipping under the earth.

The waitress brings coffee. She smiles at them.

"I was a waitress when I met your father," Barbara says. She curls fingers around the handle of a coffee cup, grins bravely at Ditch. "We're a long way from California now."

They order pancakes. They put their lips to the rounded edges of their white coffee cups, blow, sip. If she knew what he wanted, she would hand it to him. She wouldn't be able to stop herself. She would give him anything.

"I have to go away," Ditch says. "I can't —"

"Is this about your father? Do you think about him?"

"Sometimes...No...This isn't about him..."

She nods as if to demonstrate her willingness — her inability — to understand.

"You never heard from him?" Ditch says.

"That nobody? Only once. When you were seven. A post-card. No address. Nothing. From Florida. I threw it out."

"You should have kept it. You could have kept it for me."

to: debstub@debstub.com
from: andy@hotflash.net

Me and my buddy made a bet that you've got a little bit of a dung coming out of your ass. He thinks it's a shadow. I've got a lot of money rid-
ing on this. So c'mon, you dropping a load or what? Please get back to
me. By the way, great pics!

3

They face each other on the sidewalk in front of the house. Blinking twilight. Barbara just getting home from work. Debs just getting up.

This is mine, Barbara thinks to say.

But everything seems so impermanent, ripped apart and stitched back together.

Debs — feral and startled. In the evening shadows Barbara sees the creases, origami folds — ancient, impossible. She sees that Debs isn't a girl at all. *Just leave, just go away.* She wants to use the word liar.

"Where are you from?" she asks kindly. She doesn't wait for an answer. She gestures to the house — to her house — as if to say: *not from here.*

"You need help. I see that now. You need help. And you know that we can't help you."

Debs shrugs, lifts her shoulders like it's an effort.

"We can't help you," Barbara says again, slowly, convincing

herself. *We don't want to help you.*

Debs thinks she might scream. Why do they think she needs their help? Who ever bothered to help her? Not her real mother. And not this wicked witch stepmom, who thinks she's part of some fairy-tale torture, wave the magic wand, make Cinderella go away — fuck that. They think I need help. They're the ones who need help. What would you do, Debs wants to say. How would you help me?

"If you'll just..." Barbara says, her voice gone strained and desperate. She fumbles with her purse, wants to offer Debs something. Money? A withered tissue?

Barbara thinks she might be yelling. Debs has eyes the colour of sidewalk, cracked and dead, poured slabs — she's crazy, Barbara can feel it, a setting concrete, names etched into accidental permanence. We've all been crazy once. We've all been —

"I know," Debs says. She stops, though she has more to say. About straddling Ditch, taking him into her. There are no first times any more. It'll all be done, over and over. Walk away. Just walk away. You don't owe her — anybody —

Watching Debs recede, a shadow into a shadow.

What? What does she know?

Barbara hugs her purse to her.

Ditch holds a plastic bag, fabricated wrinkles thin-pressed to his body. He looks around for Knudtsen's brother, a dour man in an old black suit, a stale pallor — a cheapness — on him like a fruity aftershave. The park seems empty. November painted in grey leaves, wet garbage canvas, everything in thick wide ineffectual stripes, everything stripped bare. It isn't a nice day.

"He doesn't want us to come to his house," he says.

"So...?" Debs trills. She says it like she's having a great time. She skips ahead, stops and picks up a leaf. She shows it to him: impossibly orange and alive. He can smell her. The air not quite fresh. A stillness like a small animal. They haven't left Knudtsen's apartment in a week. Dry grass folding under their feet. He tries to smile at her. He wants her to be having a great time.

They join up with the path that circles the perimeter of the park. The park is really just a giant sloped pit. Long sets of stairs at either end. From up top, everything is half-size: grey-brown toy trees, mini-picnic tables, mini-picnics. The park is practically empty. Park or pit? Ditch wonders. Everything is two things at once. Nothing easy. Nothing simple. Everyone's at work, he thinks.

"You come here in an hour, five-thirty, six o'clock," Ditch says, "and there's dogs everywhere. This place is like a kennel, that's how many dogs there are."

"I want a little doggy," Debs sings. Ditch wants to hold her hard, hug her, smell the nape of her neck. Buy her a gerbil. First love. The way a puppy strains on a leash. Puppy love. Maybe we can, Ditch thinks. It hasn't even been a week. He'll hold on to her. Don't let go of her. Don't let her out of your sight.

"Is that him?" Debs points. An older man in a trench coat stands at the far end of the pit. "Hey," Debs waves. "Hey."

Knudtsen's brother paces around a tree, comes back into view, squints.

"He can see us," Ditch says. He's glad she's with him. It's right that she's with him. Maybe we can —

"Remember when you were a kid and you would roll down a big hill and then jump up and be all dizzy?" Debs says.

Ditch surveys the slope, the drop, he's already feeling — a little on the dizzy side. She takes a step toward the edge. He wants to tell her not to.

"Debs — " he says.

The thick nervous afternoon. A bag filled with what they call "personal effects." He holds it tight to his chest. His legs are burning. She seems so young — Lighten up, isn't that what — It's what his mother always tells him. He doesn't have any friends. His mother. He thinks too much. Everything is inside. Everything is dreams: fathers and brothers and lovers and mothers.

"Over here!" Debs yells into the echo pit. "Hey, old guy! Hey! It's my birthday." She giggles. Knudtsen's brother sees her waving, thinks he sees somebody waving. Shoves his brittle hands in his coat pockets.

"Debs, c'mon," Ditch says.

"Meet you down there," she says. Her cheeks in apples. She spirals out of view. Ditch lets his legs go.

Halfway down, he realizes what he's doing. It's not so much a hill as it is a cliff.

It was like skiing, he'll think some other time, some time later — not that he's ever been skiing. His narrow jointed knees sway, then buckle. He tumbles into an accidental somersault, sprawls through tight soil, lands on top of her. Panting.

"Mmm," Debs says, pushing against him. Ditch laughs. Kisses her. They're all right. They breathe together, a taste like moulting, decomposition, new growth. Promises. The way bodies move, get carried away with themselves.

"Maybe we can —" he starts to say. She sticks her lips to him. Something sharp jabs into the small of his back. Debs has her eyes closed, is pulling. Ditch tries to get up. Her high wire arms around him. She keeps making these little noises. An act. Groaning moaning noises. Another jab in his back. He can't believe how strong she is. He tears off her, looks up.

Knudtsen's brother, tall and wind-whipped, brandishes the umbrella. He's longer than Ditch remembers. Knudtsen was short, squat. Wasn't he? The last time Ditch saw him he was a corpse. Stretched out at the funeral, Ditch thinks. Frantically, he feels for the plastic bag, its contents, its personal effects, strewn around the grass. Debs just lies there, breathing hard, her grin smeared with wet earth, her skin translucent, the crack of her belly showing.

"Debs," Ditch says. "Hey, c'mon." He looks at Knudtsen's brother, holding his black umbrella in front of him like a sword or a shield, and tries to convey something, an apology, a distance. He scrambles to his feet. Says: "I'm — I'll — I'll just get these." He bends down, grabs yellowed letters, blotchy pictures. Another time. Another decade. The end of the afternoon. The end of a life. Ditch brushes at wet and mud.

"Just give them to me," Knudtsen's brother says, waving the sharp point of the umbrella. "You're making it worse."

Ditch smooths the crushed folder.

"They were in here."

"You should be ashamed of yourselves."

The old man's not so much stern and angry as he is sallow and sad, like a petulant child starved for attention.

He doesn't talk to his brother for forty years, Ditch thinks. If I had a brother.

Debs, thank god, doesn't say anything.

"He died alone," Ditch blurts. Abruptly, he brushes at his back, his ass covered in dust and bits of leaves and orange cinder pine needles. Knudtsen's brother stands over them, glaring. As if there's any other way to die. There's no one else in the entire park. Branches in crossed gallows. All the trees look dead.

"I tripped," Ditch says.

"Running down the hill like a damn fool," Knudtsen's brother says.

Ditch is an only child. Things might have been different. Knudtsen's brother pulls out a yellowed handkerchief, blows his nose. Looks at him as if to say: *You? You won't ever know.*

Debs holds an ancient wrinkled snapshot. Something about the faces, studied exuberance, failed youth. They remind her of certain photos, of her own photos; pretend permanence, it's all porn, in the end.

"Do you mind, young lady?" Knudtsen's brother wears black gloves.

"Want the bag too?" Debs says. She's acting like a child. This is all wrong, Ditch thinks. You've got to — respect — What would his mother say? He scuffs at beige grass.

"No, thank you," Knudtsen's brother says. He bends down, grabs the picture between two leather fingertips, holds it away from him. The wind flaps at edges. It's going to rip, Ditch thinks.

Knudtsen's brother clears his throat. The air weighs everything down. Rain, Ditch thinks. He wouldn't meet us at his house. Where he lives.

"I guess —" Ditch looks down at Debs, she's ripping up dead grass, digging in the wet earth. Dirt in the grooves of her fingers. It makes things awkward, impossible. She's alive and the rest of us are dead. We're together now, I had to bring her — I didn't want her —

— *to be alone.*

Knudtsen's brother steps away. He makes a big show of erecting his umbrella. A black blooming orchid.

Or maybe it's the opposite: She's dead and we're still alive.

"Wait," Ditch finally says. "I, you should know. He was like a father to me and —"

"Maury?"

"Mr. Knudtsen?"

"Maury."

"I —"

"A father?" The old man looks away, down at Debs, lips pursed like he's going to spit. "He was a — he wasn't even a brother."

Don't look at her, Ditch thinks. *I shouldn't have —*

The wind against skeletal black petals, mutant flower fluttering.

"The man was a...how do you say it...a lech. A leech. That man was some kind of a, of a — pervert."

Ditch says: "I don't think so."

"What he did," Knudtsen's brother says. "I couldn't ever forgive."

"Ever?" Debs says.

They look down at her, surprised. That single word spills out of her mouth, sand dissolved through a fist. Knudtsen's brother doesn't even blink. White flakes of rheum on his lips. She's going to cry, Ditch thinks. But Debs is calm, her demeanour matter-of-fact methodical — a toddler playing in a sandbox. Two pigeons. A grey patchwork squirrel, pink flesh where its tail used to be. Debs works her fingers in. Legs splayed. She's having a great time.

"You see this," Knudtsen's brother says. He holds the grubby picture, sticks it in Ditch's face. A group of young men, arms around each other. "We're the only ones that got out alive. Maury and me. We were the only ones. The rest of them — dead. Not just dead. Ashes. Burned. The war...you understand?" The picture shakes, blurs, gets wet. "So don't tell me what he was and wasn't. We're alive and they're dead and for what? So he can come to this country and forget everything. And act like a — like a —" He closes his gloved fist. The snapshot disappears, flesh against flesh. Ditch looks up at the sloped grass walls. He's at the bottom of some impossible memory. He arches his neck. The sky lapses into landscape.

Knudtsen's brother walks tentatively, primly, away. He's the younger brother, Ditch thinks. He'll go blind too.

"Well," Debs says, wiping her muddy hands on her pants, "so much for that."

"It's nothing to do with us," Ditch says.

A dog creeps low, sniffs the birthday girl.

"What do you see in that kid, anyway?"

Morts drinks again, slopping whiskey.

Debs wipes at his chin with the sleeve of her shirt. His face in her chest. He closes his eyes, leans forward.

"We'll be leaving soon," she says. "This is my last night."

In the early evening, the empty bar seems so still. A museum. Static homage to some temporary past.

She puts her hands in Morts's thinning, lank hair.

Morts shoves her away. "Go then. See if I care. Fuck off and go."

Debs stares at him, remembers a school trip to the Smithsonian, the Museum of American History, the famous sets of television shows from before she was born: *All in the Family*, *M*A*S*H*; empty behind glass. They meant nothing to her.

"I could still take you away," Morts finally says. "We could forget about this place."

Debs shrugs.

If he could, he would slap her.

"Why did you even come here?"

She pulls up the hem of her shirt. Her belly a crest of snow.

"Answer me, you little —"

"If you want, Morts, I can —"

"Just go," he says.

She lets her shirt fall.

He winces, shifts in his seat.

"Does it hurt?"

"Suzie takes care of me."

"Suzie."

Morts scowls again, pain, something else. He won't look at her again. It's her eyes. If she would just —

"You think this is what I wanted?" he says. "You think I wanted it to end up like this? You come in here, with your — you get all these kids coming down here, you think you did me a favour? We were doing better without you. I was doing better without you."

He waves his arm, as if to make the bar and her, everything, go away. Whiskey slips over the edge of his tumbler.

"Morts. You're spilling."

"Yeah," he says. "I'm a real fucking mess."

"Don't say that. C'mon, Morts. Look at me. You understand. You know me. You have to understand." She feels like she owes him something. He could have been the one.

"I might have loved you," she says.

"Really?"

She nods, blushing.

"Let's get out of here then. Forget about all this."

"Not really," she sings. She spins off, doesn't look at him. Takes the open bottle off the bar, drinks from it.

Debs kisses him like she's made a decision. She writhes on top of him, she doesn't want him to move. She reaches back and slides him in. He isn't supposed to move. He zips his hands over her birdcage breasts. She folds, wriggles up and down his long flat frame. He barely feels her. The phone rings downstairs. He hears the phone being answered, his mother's voice already distant. Debs goes hot, breaks into a sweat, bucks over him, makes him wish he could see everything, see what they look like. She cries out, then leans forward and puts her sweaty head on his shoulder. They stay like that. She's almost asleep. He's wide awake, trying to figure it out. A sixth sense, a distended shadow. In the bar. I hit Bobby. I hit Bobby and Bobby went down like a pile of shit.

Ditch walked out, didn't run. Why should he run?

Ditch thrusts into her, feels her straddled legs burning his thighs. Debs pins his arms down, lets her hair form a tent around their heads. The phone rings again, downstairs. Barbara doesn't answer it. They're alone, the two of them.

Afterwards he says: "It's your birthday?"

He doesn't even know how old she is. Certain things they don't talk about. Like how old she is, where she came from, when they'll go, where they're going. *Have you given any more thought to your future?* The police might be looking for me. How about that, Mom?

He called work, took some time off, bad, bad flu going around. Spent the last week lying in her rumpled blanket, her body cold against his. They sleep, fuck, get drunk. She'll go out for a bottle or a pack of gum and he'll lie there waiting until she comes back, hoping she won't.

The nights are long. She hates to go out. She almost never goes out.

It's winter now.

Don't let her out of your sight.

"Yeah, well," Debs shrugs.

"No, c'mon," Ditch persists. "How old?" He feels a drop in his stomach. Debs clenches, looks away.

Street-light ghosts in the dark empty room. Headlight night, evening travel, insouciant lines, permeable beams pointing — so, okay, let's go. Ditch thinks: Why not? Where are we going? What are we waiting for? They don't talk about it. His legs fold awkwardly under him.

"Hey," Debs says. "Can't we just — I've got something to celebrate with."

"What the hell," Ditch says. He's ugly now. "We've got so much to celebrate."

She comes back from the kitchen with a jug of cheap white wine. "Grabbed it from the bar," she says, putting the bottle on the floor between them. Morts is dying, might already be dead. She changes the subject: "One time it was my birthday and I wanted to make french fries, you know, like home-made. Because it was my birthday. I filled up the oil all the way to the top. The burner glowing bright red. I was such an idiot. I sliced like thirty potatoes. When I dropped them in there was a sort of splash noise then whoosh. Flames. What an idiot."

"Hey," Ditch says. He doesn't know what to say. Her stories, they're like following crumbs through a labyrinth. They're going somewhere where they don't seem to go. Just stories. It's her birthday. "Hey," he says, "You were probably little."

Debs holds the jug up to her jutting mouth. She drinks, spilling wine down her front.

Ditch could go downstairs, get them both proper wine glasses. He doesn't offer. He won't leave her. Her little world. Her rosé lips. He's pretending his mother doesn't know where he is.

She gets close, slips her tongue in. The taste is cold, sour.

"Yeah, sure," she breathes. "I was little."

He wants to tell her something, but can't think of what. So he drinks in hollow fat gulps, puts the bottle down, feels his gut rot.

Debs goes into the bathroom, locks the door.

The air is rank, sex and puddled wax. Candle burnt down to its wick. The jug of wine almost empty. Debs wakes up, pulls herself out of Ditch's arms. He doesn't believe her. *He thinks it isn't really my birthday.* Even he doesn't believe her. Not that he would ever come right out and say it. Wimp. Faggot. Pussy. Bitch. He doesn't have the balls to get mad at her. The air is acrid desire, a smoke smoggy lust. She looks down at him with something like pity. Suze was right. Poor Ditch. Look at him. Sleeping. Sleeping like a lump. Nobody tells her the truth. Nobody tells her what they really think.

"A lump, a log, a lake," Debs sings. She could kick him. She could bite him hard, rip a nipple off. Fuck him.

"Already did." She's laughing. Ditch stirs, sees her standing there.

"What're ya —?" he muffles. He's wasted.

"A lump," Debs sings. "A lump of shit."

She could kick him. What does he think — they're going

to stay up here for ever? That she loves him — needs him, hates him — is more like it. She wants someone to take control. He can't even —

"I was thinking about my father," she tells him.

Ditch props himself up, holds the bottle out to her.

"He used to touch me," Debs says.

He swallows, thinks he's going to be sick.

What's true isn't the truth. It's who we are, it's what makes us think we can be what we're not.

Debs is cold inside. Inside she's a fingerprint, she's evidence. She gets him hard, then doesn't even bother. She jumps up, pulls on her sweatpants. She finds her drugstore camera, goes over to him. "Hey, wake up. Wake the fuck up." She kicks him. He's awake. "Fucking wake up." She throws the cardboard camera at him. "Take pictures of me. Wake the fuck up and take pictures of me."

Flash: She smiles too hard, cracks her smooth face.

Flash: She yanks up her white t-shirt, shows the bottom of her breasts.

Ditch takes pictures, winds the film with his thumb. Finally he stops, says:

"What if Knudtsen was some kind of pervert?"

"Don't you get it," Debs says. "You're all perverts."

She bends over. Ditch is too drunk. His head rolls to one side. His words are blurred together, out of focus. He aims and points.

Flash: He goes blind.

Ditch wakes up thinking: One leg at a time.
He puts himself in his jeans.

Debs runs.

It feels good.

It's what she's good at.

Last resorts. Disappearances. She wasn't the one who ran away. Just waking up and waiting and waiting. Her parents, weren't they the ones? Nobody knows, she sings into the burning wind. Only I know. Her boots make no noise, she imagines leaving tracks like a bird, three claw hops, once place to another. Forget about it, everything. All of it. Clean slate. Start over. But at night she hears it, a sound like laughing, like a disc drive's empty whirring, like a security camera swivel. It's her father, watching her, waiting for her behind the shaded windows while the detectives — one thin and tall, one squat and plump — stand in the street fondling their walkie-talkies. Start over. Find somebody. Ditch is all right. But he's — he's too — doesn't believe in anything. He's not real. What else is she going to do? No fucking balls. Morts has cancer of the nuts. Otherwise she would have — Jesus. Don't think about it. Anyway, I can't go back to work — they all — they think — I'm a slut, so what? So what?

She did what she had to do. She wasn't the one who ran away.

Debs stops, closes her eyes, can't get her breath. Houses all around her, pressed tight together, people packed in them, asleep. The house where she grew up — if you could call it growing up. She's alone. No. That's not true. E-mail is real. Words are real. Pictures — he sent me — the password — print it out then burn it then eat it, he loves me, he's looking for me.

She runs with her head back, tries to see stars, just street lights and power cables, long black lines connecting the distance between one place and another. She turns a corner, smacks into someone. Bounces off like a balloon.

"What the fuck?" the stranger staggers back.

"Hey, sorry," Debs sways. She stands on her tiptoes, whispers into the man's ear: "It's my birthday." She licks his cheek.

Runs again.

She'll run with her eyes closed. Forget what she's done, who she's been. She'll throw her computer off the top of the CN Tower. Sure, why not, she's never been. Just seen it glowing, it's stupid, isn't it stupid? It glows, Daddy. It's like a big fucking glowing dildo.

Anyway, he'll never find me.

Hey, this is easy. I can go all the way around the block. C'mon now. No goddamn peeking. Keep those eyes closed.

Debs imagines she knows exactly where she is. She picks up

speed. Her toes are rotting, bleeding, rubbing against each other in scab inversions. It isn't me. It isn't my fault. Those detectives — hounding me. *Don't leave town.* I'm eighteen. I can do what I want.

She doesn't need anyone's help to disappear.

Ditch finds her. He traces the angry bruise on her forehead. Face first into a telephone pole. He doesn't have to ask: What did you think you were doing?

You close your eyes and point in some direction you can only see in your mind.

She mutters something. *Daddy.*

"It's okay, it's me, I'm going to pick you up. Take you home. It's okay."

She shifts, he barely feels her in his arms. He can't believe how light she is. She kicks her legs at the wet night.

She stinks of piss.

"Aw Jesus, Debs."

He can handle this. He can deal with this. What would his mother — I'm not her mother. And Knudtsen wasn't some kind of a —

A lovely. A pretty.

There isn't a moon. He walks slowly. His legs are tight. He wants to end it where it is. He wants his life back, he'll drive the van, save his money up, own a car, take his mom to Price Club and IKEA, buy in bulk, sip tea and watch the nightly news. Debs smells, stinks. He doesn't know what he wants.

"We just need to get out of here," he tells her.

— Mom — but she'd only —

He could put her down and walk away. Lay her out on the sidewalk like an offering. Never see her again.

He kisses her forehead. She presses into him.

In the morning Barbara thinks:
I'll throw them both out.
So what the hell am I supposed to do?

In the morning it's like nothing even happened. It's like Ditch didn't towel her off, pull her into a sweater. She was shivering, kept saying: "No no — no oh no no no." Pushing him away. Something else, something like Doggy or Daddy or Baddy.

She rolls over and puts a hand on her forehead. Starts laughing.

"Really, dahling," she drawls. "We have to stop meeting like this."

The sun cuts through the clouds and disappears. Hungover men wearing greasy beards drive the empty streets tossing newspapers on porches. The city licks its wounds. The night tells stories. Everybody listens.

Ditch finally falls asleep. Dreams of a big house, slowly filling up with grey. Debs is there, only it's someone else. Knudtsen arrives, rings the doorbell. He isn't invited. He unzips his fly and says: *So what? I'm an old man.* Some kind of earthquake happens and then everyone's standing naked in the newspaper dump. Ditch says: But there's never been an earthquake.

He blinks awake. Debs is hunched over the small computer screen. He sees tied-up shapes, pinioned bodies, wide mascara eyes — tits and whips.

He knows what his mother is going to say, finishes her sentences in his head, feels like he's cheating on a test or watching a play with the script in his lap.

"We have to —"

talk.

"You can't just do —"

whatever you feel like.

"This is my —"

house.

"You're not a —"

kid any more.

"When are you going to —"

grow up

"and start accepting —"

responsibility.

"I'll be gone —"

one day.

"And then who will —"
take care of you.
"If you don't learn how to —"
take care of yourself.
"Have you thought about your —"
future?
"You're a bright —"
kid
"and I can't stand to see you —"
throwing it all away.
"You're acting like —"
your father.
"He was a —"
drunk.
"He left us, that —"
good-for-nothing.
"And now you're —"
running around.
"And that, that —"
girl.
"It breaks my —"
heart.
"Are you planning on driving a van for the —"
rest of your life?

He stands in the kitchen and lets it all spool out in front of him, the karaoke soundtrack, his life a bad pop song nobody bothered recording.

"So," Barbara says, "what do you have to say for yourself?"

He doesn't argue with her. He isn't going to argue with her.

He hates her. It has nothing to do with her. Why does he have to hate her?

She just stands there. He refuses to — he can feel his damp thick socks, the smell of another day passing, air wafting up between them when he shifts his feet.

And his boots, stinking up the hallway.

So what? I live here too.

She ambushed him. Came home early. Before he could —

At least she hadn't caught him — them —

"I've made you an appointment," Barbara says. He looks at her, sees the way her mouth creases her face. She's old. This isn't part of the script. Pity, apprehension, disgust. I'm a bad son. I'm all she —

"What?" he says. "What are you talking about?"

"Can't you listen to me?"

Ditch shrugs. He thought he was ahead of her. He thought he knew everything she could possibly have to say.

She hands him a card.

Mary Heinz, counsellor.

He wants to turn away.

His legs burn. He just stands there.

"Someone to talk to," she says. "Ditch, it wouldn't hurt for you to talk to somebody about —"

"— my future."

"Oh, Ditch. You don't have to say it like that."

The office of Mary Heinz is dark and important. A place for matters of gravity, words weighed out the way a teller counts money. The smell of leather and pipe smoke. It's a serious smell. Ditch thinks of coffins, the dreams he's been having, Knudtsen and his mom embracing under the thick sheaves of old newspapers. What is he doing here? His problems aren't interesting, his dreams mundane. Is he so important? He isn't. He really isn't. He feels like he should have something smart to say. Some wisecrack a character uses in a novel. He doesn't read novels.

"So," he tries. "You smoke a pipe?"

"No," Mary Heinz says curtly.

He flushes.

"I should take it up, though," she finally says, her face breaking into a reluctant smile.

Ditch shrugs, relieved. He'll make her think he's something he isn't. He won't talk about his childhood.

"Well," Mary Heinz begins, speaking cautiously, surprising him.

He thought she'd be smooth, assured, instant.

"Your mother wanted you to...to see me."

"Do you know her? Does she come here? Is she your …patient?"

"Client."

"Client?"

"That's right. I'm not a doctor. I don't have patients."

"Is she your client?"

Mary Heinz seems flustered, annoyed. So that's all it takes, Ditch thinks. He can't believe it. His mother, who knows everything, the exact spacing and placing of the dessert spoon, how to say "no, thank you" when the save-the-planet charity gets you on the phone and asks for money, what to do when she feels an earthquake from the other side of the world. His mother, coming here.

"What if she is?" Mary Heinz says. "Would that bother you?"

Ditch shrugs.

"Is it that she keeps secrets from you? And you, do you keep secrets from her?"

Ditch shrugs again.

"Everybody keeps secrets."

"Okay," Mary Heinz says in a way that seems to suggest the matter is closed. She glances down at her desk; he sees her looking at her hands, holding on to them.

To keep from strangling me.

"So," Mary Heinz says. "Is it the case that these secrets are more important than you think? I mean, are they coming between you? You and your mother?"

"Not really," Ditch says. "It's nothing like that. I don't really have any, I mean."

"But you said everybody does."

"I mean, the little stuff. But I'm, I mean, not like that."

"Like what?"

"I don't have secrets. Not really. I don't do anything."

"I don't believe that."

"I'm just some guy, you know."

"I don't know, not really."

"I thought you could tell me..."

"What?"

"It's stupid."

"I'm sure it's not."

"I mean, I feel stupid, being here."

"Not at all."

"My mother wants me to go back to school."

"So," Mary Heinz says. "You're thinking about it?"

"I mean, I didn't have great grades. But I could get in, somewhere, maybe, I could, you know, get ahead."

"I'm sure you could."

Ditch shrugs. He hears a clock ticking. Is it his imagination? His mom will pay for this, he realizes. How much an hour?

"I don't really think — " his voice is sullen, louder than he intends it. "I mean, what's the difference?"

"I'm not sure I understand."

"I mean, school — it's just a possibility," he says.

"A possibility?"

"Yeah, you know, like getting a promotion. Or committing suicide."

Mary Heinz laughs.

"I see," she says.

Ditch realizes he's sweating.

"What I mean is, lots of things are possibilities."

"In your life."

"In my life."

"What else, Ditch? Tell me some other possibilities."

"I could...travel."

Mary Heinz raises her eyebrows.

"Is that on your mind? Going somewhere?"

"You seem surprised."

"That's not for me to say, really."

"Oh."

"Where would you go?"

"If I travelled?"

"Yes."

"Not, like, anywhere specific. I mean, it would just be to...get away."

"Get away from what?"

"From what? I don't know. Everything. Nothing. I told you. My life. I'm...it's..."

"Boring?"

"That's right."

"You feel directionless?"

He laughs, watches her hold on to her big hands.

"That's not exactly a secret."

"And travel, is it a direction?"

"You have to go somewhere."

"But otherwise?"

"It's more, like, looking for something. Hoping you'll find a direction, isn't it?"

"I think so, yes."

"Yeah, okay. But so what? You know. So what?"

His legs ache, his knees protruding, out of joint. He's angry, he doesn't know why he's so angry. *My mother — why did she have to — she thinks I'm — But I'm not, I'm not.*

"I mean, shit, going back to school, it's the same thing isn't it?"

"I'm not sure that's true."

Ditch looks around the room. He keeps waiting for something to happen. It's the stillness, unnerving, floating at the centre of everything. *Am I so important? I'm really not.* What is he waiting for? Something simple, the phone ringing, the door opening, an interruption.

"I'm sorry if this is making you uncomfortable," Mary Heinz says.

"Yeah, well," he tries to smile. "It's...you know."

Mary Heinz makes a face as if just noticing how full of shit he really is.

Ditch won't tell her anything.

"And this travel..." Mary Heinz says. "You'll go with friends?"

"Did my mother say that?"

"She's concerned."

"She wants me for herself."

"Is that what you think?"

"What are we really talking about here?"

"There's a...relationship?"

Ditch blushes.

"Well, yeah. Sort of."

"Sort of?"

"I mean, you know, we're just — more than — but we haven't —"

"Do you want to?"

"Uh, yeah, well, you know how it is."

Mary Heinz smiles encouragingly.

"Of course," she says.

Ditch looks away, at the landscape over her head.

"Ditch, do you think it would be a good idea? To take a trip with this...friend?"

"I don't know."

"Have you talked about it with her?"

"She wants me to."

"And what do you want?"

"I don't know. Isn't that the problem?"

"I'm not sure. Is that the problem?"

"This is stupid, you know. Maybe there isn't a problem. My life, I just —"

"You just —"

The clock ticks.

"I think about her — you know. I think about her all the time. My mother — she doesn't like her, she thinks — but I'll go crazy, you know. If I stay. If I don't — And sometimes, I have these dizzy spells and — I think — it's like —"

He's standing. He realizes he's standing.

"Can I go now?"

Morts sleeps in the back room. His breath stinks like fat meat. Bacon, Ditch thinks. Ditch watches him slip in and out. What do the dying dream about? Ditch shakes him, calls his name. He pulls him into a sitting position.

Morts opens his mouth, tries to say something. It comes out air. The pain is light now. He can stand outside, watch himself fade like an old picture. His lips in tremors.

"Morts — I can't understand you."

Ditch has a bottle, two shot glasses.

Ditch pours the shots, puts one in Morts's hand. Morts makes a fist, and Ditch guides the drink up to his cracked lips. Morts feels the hot burn spread through him, motions for another. Ditch repeats the process, guides curled fingers up to that raw mouth. Morts makes a sound like wincing. His hand doesn't feel real. Ditch has another himself. *My father was a drinker.* Morts coughs, keels over.

"Are you okay?" It's a stupid thing to say.

"Suze'll be in soon," Morts finally gasps. The liquor makes him stronger. His voice filling his ears. He shakes his head. "She's taking care of me. I'm gonna leave her the bar — I shouldn't — it's a curse."

Ditch watches him laugh. Dusky air barely swirls. The back room's a shed, a storage area, a closet. No place to die. There's an old calendar, healthy girls with big flouncy hair, double-handful tits, a blonde in a fat white parka open in the front. January 1985. Single light bulb on a string. If there was a window, Ditch thinks. What difference would it make?

"You should be in the hospital," he says.

"You should be in jail." Morts motions at the bottle. "You want another?"

Ditch grins.

They drink, sit in silence. Morts falls asleep, wakes up.

"You still here?" He's angry.

"I —" Ditch grabs on to the sides of his chair. "Sorry," he says, "I was just feeling a little —"

"Sick?" Morts laughs again, a dry throat croon. "Get out of here."

Ditch doesn't move.

"I just — I just wanted to tell you —"

"She wouldn't come herself?"

Ditch shrugs.

"Tell her I love her." Morts spits up bubbles over his stained quilt. "Tell her she was the best thing that ever happened to me."

"You'll be all right on your own?"

"Suzie's coming soon. She's got the pills. From her boy in Buffalo..."

"What should I do?"

"...They keep me comfortable...while I...cancer of the balls." Morts makes a desperate sawing motion, air through his concave fist. The jerking-off joke. He drops his arm in his lap. "At least don't...don't let her be alone."

Ditch stands. He has to hold on to something. A bit — dizzy. It could be any time. It's nine in the morning. A basement bar he used to frequent. He turns to go.

"Leave the bottle," Morts whispers.

Nine thirty-three a.m. A twenty-three-year-old man smelling of bourbon and semen. In his nostrils: the stink of urine. Beads of perspiration string out on his forehead like Christmas lights.

The bank is gaudy, festooned. Red and green bulbs syncopate on a plastic pine. It's more than a month away, Ditch thinks. He's not sure he can face waiting in line.

He waits in line. Takes eighteen hundred and thirty dollars out, closes his account. Asks for it to be converted to American currency.

The teller counts green hundreds.

Ditch shifts from leg to leg.

The teller checks his licence, his signature. Quick glances at him while she types.

Sweat on his upper lip. Tastes like bitter medicine.

Ditch grabs the cash, his receipt. Looks up at the security camera. Waves.

4

They leave at night. The bulk of the van behind them, empty space captured. Debs sits with her legs crossed. She stares out the window. Her neck, a fragile golden stem, the flower of her hair caught in passing headlights. *What is it?* Ditch wants to ask.

They're barely out of the city. Their destination isn't real. He doesn't speak. He knows it's the road, the cars lined up in slow columns, the inky scenery of brake lights and white lines in fragments. He creeps the van forward, careful to occupy space as it is allotted. He looks over at Debs as if he's stealing something. She's fixed on some point. His furtive glance.

A horn blows. Ditch stares at the side of her head. His eyes wide against the night. Cars swerve around. The van doesn't seem to be moving. Talk to me. Horns muted, disappearing down the highway. He's pressing on the gas. Isn't he pressing on the gas? What's the problem?

It's as if they're not moving. Red and orange lights leave streaks on his eyes. He feels his foot, heavy on the floor of the van. The engine roars and they hurtle forward. But Ditch stays in place. He blinks. Lines of light crowd his vision. The glowing sheaf of her hair. The immutable side of her face. Then the road sways, turns upside down. There's the blare of highway noises: swirling bleats mixed in with the swish of cars passing. He moves his lips, forms the words to tell himself — *It's okay. I'm okay. Talk to me. Somebody — What am I?* — His hand on the spinning steering wheel. Lights in orbit glittering. Hands over his eyes. My hands. My own hands. His legs tucked under him. "It's okay," he hears. "It's okay."

"I stole the van," he says. "I stole it."
"Where'd you get it?"
"It doesn't matter. From work."
"You stole it?" Debs smiles. She's delighted.
Ditch turns the key.

They stop at a fast-food place. Ditch looks greasy, done up, desperate. Debs holds his hand.

"I feel dizzy," Ditch says. "I don't know. I've never been like this."

"It'll go away. It's nothing. Take it easy. It'll pass."

"How do you know?"

"We have to keep going."

"But I can't drive. What if it happens on the highway? I could kill us. It's like being picked up and flipped over. You don't understand. It's crazy."

"It's okay. It goes away. Just relax. Drink some Coke. You're tired, the sugar, it's good for you."

He sucks through the straw. She smiles at him. The air is slick, hard to get at.

"Let's go outside," he says.

She touches his hand.

"I never got my licence," she says. "My mother wouldn't let me. We have to keep going."

He pushes against the side of the van, takes swooping breaths of parking-lot air. Everything at shifting angles.

The highway is a trap, he thinks. Stretches of road where even the shoulder disappears, no way to get off. Debs leans into him. Two bodies fold against hard metal. He closes his eyes.

He doesn't know where he is, but the smell of old newspapers is everywhere, familiar. The air is soiled, clotted and dark. Outside a truck backfires. Her head on his shoulder, the slender angle of her bare neck. The ridges of the van floor curve up against his back through the thin sleeping bag spread under them. Somewhere close, distant, the sound of cars rushing by like an angry river. He falls asleep again. Dreams of a boy buried under newspapers, dog-paddling through the basement depths of a suffocating maze.

They wake up cold.

Debs disappears under jeans, two sweaters.

It's morning, just after dawn. Ditch knows what time it is. He thinks of waiting for her, sneaking into her apartment. The way hours pass by, clustered moments, merged details, so easy to forget. He shivers, puts his hands between the crotch split of his jeans. When he speaks, he sees his breath in blocks.

"They'll know by now. The shit will be hitting the fan just about now."

Debs stares at him. Her smooth face, masked indifference. A mask. He can't help her.

"The van," Ditch tries to explain. "It's morning. They'll know I stole the van. Christ. I stole a fucking van."

She smiles then. Touches his cheek. Her finger is thin, cold like an icicle. "We'd better get going," she says. "We've got to get across the border. Turn the engine on. It's cold."

"You're freezing." Her fluttering hands, shivering organs, the wings of a fragile insect. Early light through soft fresh skin. Ditch reaches, grabs her hands. He doesn't care about the truth. The truth doesn't matter. "Here. Let me warm them up."

She pulls away.

"We have to get going. We don't have time for this."

Her face held in place by the possibility of collapse. He's never seen her cry.

The road curves under him. Slipping embankment. Faded guardrail. Green sign, white numerals. The van floats, tips, clings to pavement. Ditch stares at the dashboard. A sudden plunge. He thinks to grab the steering wheel. *But I'm already driving.* Driving through a wave, a soupy bottomless dump, wet papers moulting, holding on, sucking in. His feet jerk, working the pedals. He doesn't feel them. He doesn't feel anything. He's done things now, things he never meant to do, things he can't take back. And would he take them back? It doesn't really matter. It's beyond that now. It's beyond just feeling. He moves out into the highway, hunched forward. Over the wheel, eyes straight ahead. He looks in any direction. He doesn't look. Heart thick against his chest. Speeding into the receding morning. Jesus — it's morning. "They want to kill him," Debs is saying. "But you believe me, don't you? You know that he's not the kind of man who could do those things." Ditch drives, doesn't know what to say. He sees her feet on the dashboard. Her toes dripping.

"I'm all right," he interrupts.

She looks at him, surprised.

The van rattles. The windows shake. Grey air, grey sky, grey road, grey eyes.

"You're all right," she agrees.

"Here," Debs says, "This one. This line."

Surveillance cameras, police cars, barriers. Uniformed officers circle, expectant vultures. Debs squeezes the bones in his hand.

He aims the van at a distant customs hut. The sun behind the clouds. They all look the same to him. The heater belches lukewarm air. A reluctant morning. Debs brushes her hair. Smooths a touch of red lipstick on her thin pale-pink lips. Ditch thinks: I have to call my mother; she's alone now.

The United States of America.

Morts dies in a shuddering slump of relief. Suzie puts her shirt back on, takes the glass out of his hands, calls for an ambulance.

"I forgot my purse, officer." Debs quivers her lips in a pout. "My ID was in it, officer, everything. Please don't make us go all the way back to Toronto. *Pleeeze.*"

Customs guy leans into the window for a better look. Ditch pressed against the seat, his identification in hand. Customs guy sighs, makes a mental note of Debs's nickel nipples, turgid currency under a thin white undershirt. Something to drink to.

Something to jack off to in a customs stall. Debs blinks languorously.

Then they're through.

"Put the window up," she says. "I'm fucking freezing."

He rolls up his window. He stares past the dirty glass.

"It looks the same," Ditch says.

Debs's eyes are wide returning circles. Ditch sees them, inescapable. She can go anywhere, it would be the same anywhere, her freedom a prison on her.

"Welcome to Buffalo," she laughs.

"When this is — over," he says, "let's keep going. Let's drive to California. I want to find the diner where my mom used to work. Where my mom met my dad."

"What for?

"I —"

She leans over, kisses him on the cheek. She likes the idea of it.

"Buffalo," he says, his eyes wide. They've gotten away with something. It's more important than the two of them. Where they might be going, where they've been. If she's crazy, she's crazy. (That's what he tells them. Later. He tells them that he's not sure it matters.) The city slides by. He's not sure what matters. Rooftops and broken windows reach out to the raised expressway in supplication.

They see a sign: Liquor and Beer Barn.

"Pull off," Debs says.

They wind down from the expressway into some crumbling section of the city.

Ditch steps out of the van. The city is vague, familiar. Under the clouds, the neon flashing beacon: a smiling man tipping a bottle into his mouth over and over again. Up close, the sign's lights dim, blur, spread over everything. Ditch is a speck in a painting. He looks around for Debs, but she's gone ahead or has been left behind. The parking lot divides into atoms. The sky compresses. He sees everything too close.

I'm a drinker too now, Daddy —

A big man in cowboy boots says: "Ya'lright?" Liquor super-store parking-lot security. He smiles down at Ditch as if they're just joking around.

Then Ditch is standing under the awning of the Liquor and Beer Barn. Debs leans against the wall. She holds a brown paper bag under her arms. She's trying to stay steady. She slips. Ditch grabs her.

"It's just," she says, smiling gently, "I did something to my feet. I'm sorry. I shouldn't have." He picks her up. She grips the brown paper bag like a life preserver. Blood drips off the heel of her boot. Ditch walks in a circle, expanding against his own confusion. He finds the van. He fumbles for the keys, half drops Debs. Her feet touch the ground. She moans.

"We're fine," Ditch says. "She's just —"

Security nods encouragingly.

It gets darker. The tipping neon figure, his stomach glowing where the booze hits, light bulb explosions in flashbulb bombs. Take a picture here. Remember this. He starts the engine. He switches on the headlights. Liquor and Beer Barn. It's dark. Always open. He can't see. 24 Hours.

It never occurred to him that they might get lost.

He aims the van south, out of the city. He drives narrow deserted streets. Hours later, the road widens past green and grey houses, red shutters, brown lawns. The van is slow, a burden, a beast he has to urge forward.

The roads link into each other like a child's toy.

Debs sleeps, her mutilated feet tucked under her, stork legs bent into a fragile impermanent prayer; that, together, they will somehow find their way through the inky night.

I laughed. The road was dark. There were no signs. I didn't see any signs. It was snowing. It must have started snowing. I felt safe in the van. I stared out into the snow coming down and pretended that Ditch was my husband, that he loved me and would always take care of me. I held his hand. He drove slowly, hunched forward. I told him that I could see the snowflakes smashing into the windshield one flake at a time. Then I told him about Mr. Leblanc, the French Canadian always trying to shovel the snow, the snow always melting before he could shovel it. We laughed.

Ditch said we had to find a gas station soon. Ditch says gas the funny way, with an s at the end. I kept telling him to say gas and laughing. Say gas, I said. Say house. I couldn't stop laughing. I wasn't cold any more. He was cute, all worried like that. I unzipped his pants and lowered my face. Don't worry so much, I wanted to say. We skidded off the road. Now he was talking, telling me how much he loved me. I'll save your father, he said. I'll do anything. He closed his eyes. It was silly. He closed his eyes. We imagined we were somewhere else. His thrusts gagging me.

Ditch's door was jammed. He pulled himself over me and pushed my door open. We fell into the snow. There was already a lot of snow on the ground. I was laughing. I couldn't help it. It didn't matter. Nothing mattered. Ditch said: It's stolen anyway. He pulled me up. We climbed out onto the road. It was dark, probably the darkest I've ever seen. I guess we could have been drunker than I thought. My feet stung, but once we started walking I couldn't feel anything.

I fell 20 or 30 times before he picked me up. It was a ten-minute walk to the nearest house. Porch lights on. People are friendly, I kept thinking, giggling. It took us hours. Ditch stumbled and we both fell and I started laughing. My mouth tasted dry and fruity. They make it out of potatoes, you know. But, Daddy, you know that. My feet were totally frozen.

We were standing on the porch. Ditch was knocking and there was a dog inside going totally crazy. Who's out there? a man yelled. Who the hell is out there? Ditch didn't say anything. He looked down at me, in his arms, it felt so good in his arms. It's just us, I said like an idiot. I guess the sound of a girl's voice did it though because the door opened a crack. Our car ran off the road, I said. We saw your light. Please, if we could just come in. We're freezing to death. The man was peering, like he was trying to see what was behind us or something. Finally he opened the door. He was old. So was the dog. I almost laughed when I saw the dog. They looked the same, the man and the dog. Behind them on the stairs a lady stood all wrapped up in her housecoat. She looked like she was going to fall right over. She looked afraid.

debstub@debstub.com

Password Accepted:

Loading 642 new e-mail messages...

"I'm Debs and this is my brother Ditch."

The couple lean in to look at what they can't see. Their heads bob slowly, lips cupped to taste the strange new names.

"We're from Maryland. Mary-land. Near Washington, D.C."

The old woman whispers to the man.

He nods, looks proudly at Debs.

"We have cousins in Maryland."

It smells, Ditch thinks. He peers into the living room.

They brush elbows on a plastic-covered loveseat. The living room on them like weather.

"Mother says you'll stay the night in the guest room. She'll have a nice breakfast for you in the morning. And then you'll be on your way."

Debs's pleated smile. The old man's soft face, kind and pleading. The diffuse light. Ditch keeps blinking, falling asleep.

"Thank you, sir," Debs purrs.

"Please," the old man says, eyeing her. "It's Robert. Bob."

A bulb behind a frosted fixture. Snow in thick drifts. The van on its side slowly disappearing.

"Mother says you'll be very comfortable. The bed's already made up."

The huge room, everything out of proportion, this museum of aging, this sanctuary of dust, a gruesome exhibit.

"Of course," Bob is saying, "Mother can make up the couch for your brother."

"Oh no," Debs says, jumping up. "We couldn't ask any more of you. We'll be fine in the guest room. Really, it's too much — and we're both so very tired."

She glares at Ditch. He heaves himself forward, legs shaking. I crashed the van. We crashed it. In her mouth. These old people. He feels himself getting hard. He looks over their heads.

Over their shrivelled heads: a spinning future, the horizon like a stone marker orbiting two graves. Musty newspaper rustling down a dark hallway.

The bed is an artifact. Cones of dust. A window exposing the bare back of the property. The sky in charcoal, the snow in bursts, sheeting off the top of a dilapidated garage.

He holds her, presses against her, feels her bones. Her body almost familiar. It's true: he doesn't love her. Or she doesn't love him. But there are other things, other ways to understand what it is between them. Debs's face in the cleft of his shoulder, her soft chin, angular against his protruding clavicle.

"They're blind," he says. He thinks he's shouting. "They're both almost blind."

He wraps around her. It is winter now, not suddenly, but purposefully. A season like an ending. Wherever they are, whatever happens next, Ditch knows it's almost over. Debs slips out of his arms, peers through the grime of the guest-room window.

"Look, that garage out there. I bet they've got a car. They probably never use it. Maybe we could...borrow it."

She giggles.

"Debs, c'mon," Ditch says. He can hear himself whining. Why am I — I sound like — some kind of — "We can't, I mean, Jesus...I crashed the fucking van..."

"Can you imagine the old man driving? We'll be doing them a favour. We'll be saving his life."

"What are you talking about? We can't —"

"Anyway, you already stole a van. And we have to keep going. We have to leave in the morning."

She pulls off her wet sweater, the thin white shirt under it, her ribs like boards in a worn wood floor. Ditch opens his mouth just for something to do. He says something, anything. Whatever she wants him to say: It'll be okay or It's all right or Calm down now. She's shivering. His body leads him. His words flow out of him in deflated bubbles. Veins writhing in the cords of his neck.

Her hands dropping his pants.

Remember my bedroom?

I thought it was so great. All those different shades of pink. A real girlie room. So fucking girlie. Remember I had it redecorated when I was 16? You paid for everything. I picked out the pink drapes with the frills.

Remember?

I've never worked a day in my life.

Here it is, I told him. The whole of my childhood.

I opened my legs. He licked his lips.

Ditch sits up, the sound of dripping, the melt of an early snow. The sun in the room, a slanted beacon, a thick occupation of air.

"Hey. Debs. It's late."

"Shhhh. Lie down now. I'll take care of it. Come back to bed, you."

The scratchy blanket between them. He feels for her and she opens herself.

"Not there," she says. "There."

How much farther can they go?

"Like that. Just like that."

She tells him with her body, tunnelling under the clearing snow, under the muddy patches. He knows everything there is to know about her. They aren't far. She will get them there. He's just the witness, the co-pilot, the accomplice, the intern, the sacrifice, the cipher. They come together and he pulls out slowly. He kisses the swell of her belly. Pulling out. Pulling out. Her knees. Her thighs. He bends over her feet like he can't believe it. White cotton socks dried with blood.

"They don't hurt." She smiles.

They dress in damp clothes. Last night, a dream, Ditch thinks. The dump, the suffocating air, back to work, the way he starts each day again, incomprehensible possibilities, a fresh light through a window. Dirty snow bound tight to the earth.

Ditch sits hunched over the kitchen table. A huge plate of food in front of him, the real country breakfast Bob promised. Mother's special country breakfast.

"It's been years," the old man keeps saying. "How long has it been, Mother? How long? Years since we sat down to a breakfast like this." Bob looks sad. His face stiff margarine.

The food smells good. Ditch turns his neck, stares out the window. His fork is crusted with a white flaky coating. His knife is spotted with rust. Eggs and bacon and biscuits and gravy and home fries. A coffee cup stained on the side, something dried on the rim, the tattooed reminder of some other morning. Ditch imagines the old guy's lips in trembling ascent, thin brown liquid spilling down his chin. He watches the woman move around the kitchen. She creeps to the sink with a large cast-iron pan. Her hands are thin, shaking. She can barely hold the dishcloth. She squints down at the pan, dunks it in soapy water, pauses uncertainly as if recalling the imprint of her actions. Her hands slowly fishing the pan out and setting it on the dish rack. Ditch observes soap clusters and grease clumps oozing down the scratched black metal. Across from him, Debs eats steadily.

A watery nose presses against his hand. The ancient dog, its pleading eyes veiled and stubborn. He takes a piece of bacon off his plate, brings it under the table to the dog's snuffling nose. The animal sighs deeply, sits down between Ditch's legs, sniffs the meat, makes himself comfortable. Eat it, Ditch thinks, please eat it. One more lingering sniff. Ditch feels hot breath on his fingers, the meat devoured. He loads his filthy fork with egg. They're blind. They can't see. Remember your manners. Mom. I'm —

My manners —

He feeds the dog his breakfast. The woman stands by the sink, her hands inert in fetid dishwater. The old man tells stories, the big war, the end of the old ways, the way it used to be. Debs takes bites from her toast, smiles cutely, leans forward, lets Bob smell her. She's in the white undershirt again, her body insatiable, pressing against the thin material. He's too old, Ditch thinks, watching as if from a great distance. He won't care. Debs flips her hair. The dog licks his fingers clean. He is embarrassed for her, for himself. Bob pulls a fat key ring from his belt, takes off one tarnished key. He turns to Ditch, says something about the brakes or the lights or the slippery roads. That's it, Ditch thinks. He nods. It's that easy. There are blind old people and liars and beautiful girls chewing pensively on strips of bacon. I don't have to do this.

He takes the keys from Bob. Says thank you. Bob smiles. Ditch and her are siblings, their longing for what they don't know bringing them together in some desperate incest. The old woman mutters something in the air and Bob shakes his head in anger. He doesn't translate what she says. Debs grins a tight line. Ditch does things from an easy distance. He waves goodbye. He feels his head tilt, a fake smile, a weight trapped in his skull. At least they have each other. At least they're not alone. The dog hunched over, vomiting home fries.

At a certain point, it never stops mattering.

They drive for an hour, a day, a week, a month. Ditch can't keep track: a route he doesn't know; a delivery he won't get rid of. *Drop it off. Pick it up.*

Ditch pulls the car over, and Debs rolls down the window, asks a stranger for directions. These men — they're always men — tend to linger, peering past the window, elaborating in loud voices on just which gas station to turn left at, and which Route 33 South is the right Route 33 South, because you know, Miss, there are two, and it gets real confusing, Miss.

Ditch looks straight ahead, nods, doesn't hear a word.

There are days when they don't speak at all.

Debs thrashes in her sleep. Ditch can't remember the last time she was awake. He steals glances at her, the wagon drifting to the right. She's sweating. He puts a hand on her forehead. Her white skin wormy and damp. So what's he supposed to do? He thinks about pulling over. He thinks about the blue H rectangles they occasionally pass, arrows pointing, *Emergency*.

She wouldn't like that.

But he can't let her —

"Debs, hey, Debs."

He shakes her.

Ditch holds Debs in the parking lot. Ambulances come and go. He can't wake her up. She's getting worse. Her breathing, usually soft and methodical, comes out ragged and irregular. Harsh gasps fill the cab of the wagon. He thinks of a childhood fever, his mother holding his head as he hallucinates being pulled under giant tractors, buses, steamrollers — wheels.

He watches the ambulances. The way they blunder up to the emergency double doors and disgorge their charges, never in a hurry, no one rushing or yelling, just the muted percussion of engines. He falls asleep to the sound of stretchers unfolding, his chin lost in her soft thin hair.

He dreams about newspapers, unloading stacks, throwing them out into the vast dump, a big grin on his face. He isn't driving the van, it's the station wagon that has to be emptied, newspapers bursting out the back door, falling out the open windows. The wagon belongs to Ditch, was left to him in Knudtsen's will. Ditch feels bad about using it for work. So he's unloading it for the last time, smiling as he labours, thinking, this is it. The last time.

When he wakes up, she's sweating and shivering, her skin scalding to touch. He has a hard-on. Her chest heaving. He stretches her lengthwise across the front seat of the car, backs out into the empty parking lot. The day is grey, dark. He carefully pulls off her boots. Debs groans, kicks. She screams when he unrolls a sock, her eyes flashing open, pupils floating.

He doesn't have to look. He can smell it.

What else can he do? He knows it's a mistake. She can't just — I can't just — He carries her in his arms.

A tired woman in a pink uniform has him put her on a stretcher.

"It's okay," he says. "She doesn't weigh much." He says it like it's funny. He says it like he's making a joke. *Why say that?* Ditch holds her boot, her sock. A nurse comes, looks at him, shakes her head. Wheels Debs away.

I'll never see her again, Ditch thinks suddenly. Relief blossoming in his throat.

The woman wearing pink crepe paper, deep rustling creases, sits Ditch down in her cubicle, taps at the keys on her computer.

"Name?"

"Ditch."

"Her name, please."

"Debs —"

"Last name?"

"Uh, I don't know, I'm not sure."

"You don't know?"

"Uh...William. It's William. I'm, you see, we just —"

"Does she have insurance, this Debs William?"

"I don't know."

"You don't know much, do you?"

"She's rich, I think. I mean, her parents are rich."

"Her parents. And there names are?"

"—"

"What's your name again?"

"Ditch."

"And your surname is?"

"Look, I'm just a friend. I barely —"

"Your last name please?"

"I'm just giving her a lift. A lift home. When all of a sudden she —"

"What's her address?"

"Her address?"

"Home address."

"I'm, I don't know — Because, you see —"

"But you were taking her home."

"You don't have to believe me."

"How old is this...Debs?"

"I've never been to her place. She was...directing me."

"Obviously."

Ditch makes fists, shifts in his plastic seat. The cubicle swallows him, his interrogator's pink paper dress rustles and licks like a dry tongue. He has that feeling, he's been here before, or else he'll be back again. So what if he doesn't know her name? He's made a mistake. He should still be driving.

He puts his arms out to steady himself. Thinks of his mother: *Earthquake.*

"Excuse me? Is there a — problem?"

Nothing. He shakes his head. "I just — it's nothing."

"Why don't you tell me *your* name," the receptionist says.

"I'm just a friend," Ditch says. He picks at his t-shirt. He's sweating. "Warm," he says. He smiles hopefully.

"Wait here," she says.

He gets up and leaves.

Outside, he walks quickly, head down, following the sidewalk. He comes to a clump of stores, a thin parking lot. The pizza place is closed. He's almost out of money. He goes into a bargain clothing outlet festooned with fluorescent cardboard For Sale signs. It's all for sale. The whole world, discounted. Moving slowly through the heaps of cheap garments sewn in poor countries, he finds what he's looking for. Black socks, thin and stretchy, girl's socks. He fondles the fabric between his thumb and his finger. There are no other shoppers, just him and the cashier. In a few months, the store will be closed, its wall of cheap sweatsuits repossessed, its bin of white polka-dot panties dumped on the street, picked through, plundered. He buys the socks.

At the convenience store next door he gets a can of ginger ale. Drinks it down. It tastes like metal. They'll feed her; of course they will, she's so thin.

He holds on to his tiny plastic bag of little socks. The grey morning starts to drizzle. The pizza place is still closed. I'll get home and keep seeing this place. Keep imagining it.

He thinks about leaving:

The car's in the lot. What if they're looking for me?

They aren't looking for him.

He shakes the last drops of liquid into his throat. Drops the can on the sidewalk in front of the convenience store. The noise makes him jump. He puts his hands in his pockets. Looks around. The woman in pink paper just doing her job. Just trying to do her job. She could be my mom. Ditch tries to picture his mom in a pink outfit. He can't do it.

He only did what he had to. I don't even know her last name. He won't remember the way her feet smelled. Why should I? Why would I?

Clutching his bag, he walks back to the hospital, suddenly, inexplicably, happy.

Debs is waiting for him in the station wagon. She brushes her hair in short strokes, pouts at the dashboard mirror.

"Ditch!" she says. She smiles for him.

"Hey," he says, "I got you these."

"Perfect," she says. They look down at her feet, freshly bandaged.

"They gave me a needle. Then I checked out." Debs giggles.

"But —"

"The back way, you know."

"Oh," Ditch says. He starts the car. "We should...go."

She leans over, kisses him. Her mouth tastes fresh, new.

They move past truck-stop rest areas and clusters of fast-food arches and sleepy bedroom communities partially occupied by balding men and lank-haired women who tell you that the city isn't that far, you can see it if you look for it, a series of off-ramps pointing downtown, lights flickering below the overpass, prefab rows of houses clumping on the edges of the highway, pointing the way, roofs rattling as eighteen-wheelers speed by on their journeys to and from the heartland bearing burdens of canola and sheets of plywood and toys for the children.

Ditch drives past everything, not looking, not daring to look. Keep your eyes ahead. Keep your eyes on the distance. He feels a kind of dread every time a highway turns into another. He takes the station wagon deeper into it, the past an interlocking trance, future exits.

He tells himself he'll call home. He tells himself that none of it matters — something that happened. Just something that happened.

But the way he was, the way he thinks he was — he won't ever get it back.

"Debs," he says. "Hey, Debs?"

She's dozing again, not sick, but exhausted, saving her energy, saving herself.

"Which way should we —?"

"...Whichever..."

She shifts against her seat, the long bow of her neck a perfect arc, her chin bouncing lightly against her chest.

"You're so beautiful," Ditch says. He feels a spell coming on. Grips the wheel. Lets it happen.

There's nowhere to stop. How can he stop? He's in her world now, gathering speed, a spinning porn-site smile, perpetual motion frozen in mid-fuck, mesmerizing, no time to get off, no time for anything but the ride. He thinks of the house, frantic eyes peeking through shutters, pupils in twisting revolutions.

I'll marry her, he thinks, though he can't imagine saying it. Sure, why not? If he stopped, her world would stop too, and the air, suddenly thick and grainy like an image flickering half formed on the screen, would crush them both.

He shivers, doesn't touch her. He can't imagine her. He can't not imagine her. He pretends to keep going.

"So, can you tell us what happened?"

"You already asked me that."

"Can you tell us again what happened?"

"When we got there I was like — what the hell? We can't go in there. But Debs kept saying, 'They're expecting us. C'mon, they're expecting us.'"

"And were they?"

"They were."

Ditch remembers crouching next to her in the cold empty apartment. He remembers thinking of Knudtsen, old bones and a sheaf full of fading monotone pictures, so different, so much the same indelible record. The texture of the image. The way it forms in layers, like a recollected dream.

But there was something real about it.

A rustle in the bushes.

A frantic piercing scream, then a frantic piercing silence.

He wants to eat a chicken sandwich the way his mother makes it. He wants mayonnaise to drip out of the corners of his mouth. He wants the onions to make his tongue go bumpy.

He isn't hungry.

There was something real about it. The kaleidoscope halo of the cruiser parked out front.

A kind of violence, a torture. Being half in and half out of the picture.

What was the last thing he heard her say? —

Am I under arrest, officer?

Debs back in the tub then, like she never left it. Her cleft smoothed to a baby-oil shine, wet and gleaming, a reflection.

That's the way they found her.

"I'm eighteen. I don't know where he is. I haven't heard from either of them. Can you imagine it? It's been weeks. I haven't heard from anyone. I already told you I don't know."

My hands on my hips. They were staring at my t-shirt. Through my t-shirt.

What don't I know? The cool morning air against the insides of my arms. (One of them fucking me, the other sticking his dick in my mouth.)

"He didn't do anything anyway," I said. "And if he did, she deserved it."

They shifted, adjusted holsters and boxer shorts.

"I didn't have a boyfriend," I breathed. "At the time."

What do you do with it? With the pictures that have no history, no home, no dusty photo album to pull out on rainy days and show the cousins visiting from overseas and the children and the children's children?

Ditch connects the dots, forms an image with no connection: the girl he thought he needed to love; the father he thought he could keep on imagining.

A glove grabbed her wrist. White against white skin.
The other cleared his throat in a soft groan.
"Don't go anywhere, Princess."
She locked the door and went upstairs.

Or maybe this is the last thing he remembers:

Ditch turns the car off. In the sudden silence, Debs flutters her hands, doesn't wake up.

She's asleep again, curled into herself. A newborn. A baby.

Ditch rolls down the window. The air is wet and thick, not hot but rich, the way he imagined it would be. They're close. They've outrun winter. They've outrun everything. Ditch lets himself fall against the wheel and close his eyes, but only for a second. Just breathe, he tells himself. Just keep breathing.

The plan is to get out. The plan is to escape, to admit to himself what kind of mistakes he's capable of.

He stands outside the car, looks in. It's that simple. His legs, not quite trembling, but not still either, as if struggling to support him.

He gently presses the door closed, thinks of dust and old people, what you can't see.

In the parking lot, the tinny chorus of new country

reduced to something more like crickets rubbing against each other. He has to remind himself: this isn't summer.

He keeps breathing, jumps up and down, swings his arms above his head. His thighs burn, muscles hot under his skin, he thinks of the route; it's the same now, isn't it? — the route doesn't change, Carla serving him a sandwich, the usual, Good Time Donuts. He'll leave now, creep away, get a ride up this twisting country road, the nearest town, he doesn't know where he is, pathetic, he knows, he hardly has any money left, so what is he supposed to do? He hears himself explaining it, how it happened, how it didn't happen. Or else he could — maybe Debs — she seems to have — pays for the gas, the food — not that she eats anything, I could — no — she'll — I have to — call — my mother would wire me the money, I could get her to — pathetic, he knows, he knows. But he has to —

Last chance, he thinks. He runs a hand against the bare skin of his arm, feels the goosebumps.

Inside, the tavern is familiar, shadows cast by the glare of the Budweiser jukebox. Fat men on stools, a couple shuffling against each other in a huddled embrace. Ditch goes to the bar, orders a beer. He sips at it, can't believe how good it tastes. He's hungry, alert, alive. Feels his bones dig out of him, the tension of his muscles in taut sheets, he feels like he could happen, like what happened — it was nothing, he could rip apart at any minute, last chance, he can't believe how good it feels.

He wants that chicken sandwich. The way his mom makes it, with the mayonnaise.

Pathetic, he knows.

But he's decided. He's made up his mind.

He looks around for the phone. Pretends to be cool. Doesn't want to have to hurry. After all, she's — I've — made up my —

Asks the bartender. She gives him a shy smile, points to a wooden facsimile of a covered wagon.

"Bob's pride and joy," she sighs.

Bob's Roadhouse flashes the sign over the bar.

Ditch smiles back. Asks for another beer. Sure, why not? Bob is friendly. He built his own phone booth. The little things. The details. Aren't they what matters? The things no one ever forgets. He's trying not to rush. Trying not to show it. He drinks, feels the liquid hit bottom.

Opens the door of the chuckwagon, climbs in. Feels like everyone knows. Everyone's looking at him.

Nobody looks at him.

Polished wood bench long enough for two. Ceiling of slated lacquered wood pressing down. Like a coffin, Ditch thinks. Puts his beer on the running board. Doesn't pick up the phone. Stares guiltily through the tiny window. A flashing neon sign over an empty buffet table.

Beef Bar.

Picks his beer up again. Puts it down. And starts to shake.

He's in Bob's coffin. The receiver, cold dead plastic, doesn't feel like anything in his big empty hands.

He's numb from thinking about it. Can't seem to make it happen. There's the urgency, the way his heart beats and he breathes and his legs shiver like he's trying to cling to the face of a cliff. But there's also what he can't make happen. More than anything, he wants to. What are you doing? Isn't this what you —

Calm down. Beef Bar. Chuckwagon phone booth.

"Can I help you?" the operator says. "Hello?"

"I'd like to...I'd like to..."

"Yes? How can I help you?"

"It's...a collect call...please."

His voice outside him. His body a life preserver, swimming him along, keeping him floating.

He has to —

He tries to get his beer, his mouth dry, no taste.

Knocks it over, the foamy suds soaking through his jeans, cold on the hot muscle of his thigh. He doesn't feel it.

"Collect call from...Ditch," he hears the operator say. "Will you accept the charges?"

"Yes," his mother says. That's all she says. There's a long-distance silence. Nothing he can think of will make it go away. Tiny bubbles popping on the seam of his jeans.

Then his mother says: "The police are looking for you."

Debs climbs into the booth, laughs out loud:

"Who ya calling?"

She puts a hand on the wet spot.

"It was, I can't explain it."

"Would you describe it as a dream? Could you say you were in a dreamlike state?"

"I don't know what you mean."

"Like a dream? We mean, was it like a dream? You do have dreams?"

"It wasn't a dream. It was real, okay?"

"Can you tell us about that?"

Most of the time it's warm. Spring, summer, fall. The Parent takes her to fancy beach condominiums for vacations. They're on vacation from vacation.

"Cost me a fucking fortune," the Parent says, her ample body dwarfed by a huge window overlooking the Atlantic. She always wears a chiffon skin-coloured robe over a black bikini bulging.

Debs keeps asking about him.

"Your father? A sick man. He's a sick man."

Debs sees: hospitals, nurses, stethoscopes, bright wide halls so white they glow.

"Can I visit him, Mommy?"

The Parent doesn't even look over. "Shut up, won't you? Christ, what a headache."

Iced tea on the balcony. Below them, glistening figures in states of undress spread out on beach towels. The smell of coconut oil and ocean. Abruptly, the Parent stands up, crams her cigarette into the ashtray.

"Go change into your bathing suit."

"Why?"

"You're going out."

The beach is crowded. The sun shimmers in hazy waves. I squint my eyes shut, rub them with my fists. I can't tell where the sand ends and the water begins. I stand with the ocean to my back feeling the splash over my salt-pale legs. The swells are huge. I look back at the strip of resort condominiums. I wave, flap my arms in the air. The air is heavy. A father grabs his little girl and bounces her into the waves then up down against the blue sky. She laughs, clings to him, starts to cry.

My pink bathing suit hangs off me like it's trying to slip away.

We went every summer. Maybe we only went one summer.

I open the door to the condo. Ocean wind.

Is he dead? I yell.

The sound of gulls crying. The sound of muffled bodies.

The Parent says: "How about a bloody nose?"

Debs goes upstairs. Locks the door to the bathroom. Drops her pants and underwear. Climbs up on the toilet, turns around slowly, pulls her neck over her shoulder, trying to see her ass in the mirror.

Is it perfect?

Her ass (at the time).

Twin slopes. Fresh. Like the fruit from the pear tree in the backyard.

I can't even drive. I'm afraid to drive.

She wants me out of the house. She wants my face all adult in laminated plastic. She wants me grown up. She wants me responsible. (Then she could do anything, one woman to another, she wants me.)

All the other kids. How about a bloody —

That's what she always said.

Limp and passive — a little girl in her bathing suit — it was the picture of her Ditch never saw, a holiday snapshot forgotten in the sun.

"Can you tell us what happened? Can you try and tell us what happened?"

Ditch shakes his head.

"It's not — I don't — it wasn't like that."

"What was it like? Can you tell us?"

" — "

"We want you to help us. Will you let us help you?"

"I — you don't — haven't you ever been sorry? Haven't you ever wished something hadn't happened even though you could see that no matter what, no matter what you did, it would have happened?"

"What happened?"

"I don't —"

"You stole a van. Can you tell us why?"

"You're not —"

"We're waiting."

"— listening."

"People were hurt. You were hurt. Do you remember?"

"Who was hurt?"

"Why don't you tell us?"

"Who was hurt?"

"Don't you know?"

"I don't know."

"But you were there. Can't you tell us what happened?"

"—"

"You think we would all be here now if no one was hurt?"

"Who was hurt?"

"You're yelling. Can you tell us why?"

At a certain point, he thought he imagined it.

Lying there in that hospital bed.

The whole thing, over and over again, like rewinding the nudie bits of a movie, playing them back in grainy slow-mo, playing it back — different, but not necessarily better.

How much did he know? How much did he have to know?

You have to stop thinking about it. What good does it do to think about it?

They couldn't charge him. They kept him until he was strong enough and then they brought him in for questioning, two, three, four times. But they couldn't charge him.

He didn't tell them, anyway, what he thought he knew for sure. The way things looked, how the night made it last longer, what it was like to be alive in that basement, his legs tied down in front of him, the way he was locked in place, but free of feeling, numb from the waist down.

He dreamed of her. Not nightmares. Told himself: she could have been real.

Set the scene, he kept thinking: the rotten smell of cheap wine, the glare of the flash making him blink, her distant voice: *Take pictures of me, you fuck. Take pictures of me now.*

And later the warm patch where she pissed through her jeans. And the promise to take care of her.

But he couldn't take care of her.

It's all in those pictures.

Wherever they are.

He didn't tell them about the snapshots. How clear she seemed through the eye of the camera.

Didn't he see them once? Giant on the screen, scrolling down and filling in, slowly. Didn't he see them?

They let him go. After a while. He didn't tell them anything.

About the slow creak of the basement furnace. About the way the days didn't pass.

All the days were nights.

He shuts his eyes and smells it.

Or else it's just his seat on the bus: one row up from the toilet.

"I'm not crazy."

"No one's saying you're crazy."

"I'm not crazy."

"But you were feeling a little —"

"You don't know how I was feeling."

"Let's start again. Can we start again?"

"—"

"Before you left home. Days before you left home. You saw a...professional. You saw one...Mary Heinz?"

"That has nothing do to with —"

"Can you tell us what you talked about?"

Go ahead, he thinks to himself. If you know so much. Go ahead. You tell me. What did they look like? Describe them.

The one with her shirt pulled up, just a glacier of flesh, smooth, impossible. That was the one he remembered.

Were there ever any pictures?

A whole roll.

The one with her head moving out of the frame, a smear of shifting features, a house he was pretty sure he had never seen before, if she had stood still he could have held on to her, he could have helped her.

"Can you tell her I —"
"Sure, kid, we can tell her. Do you want to write it down?"
"Forget it. Forget about it."

They wanted to know if he was her pimp. Did he help her? Did he take pictures of her? Did he run the website? Did he arrange for meetings between like-minded parties? Who took the pictures? Who put them up there? It didn't just happen by itself.

She kept saying: "C'mon big boy. Take fucking pictures of me."

That was before. Or was it after?

She knew they wouldn't last. Pictures don't mean anything.

The bus takes him to California.

He buys a postcard and stands in the post office with a borrowed pen.

5

A baby gets born, keeps quiet, does what he's told. One day he smells the night. The night is simple. The dark concedes a destination. Ditch is piloting a rusted station wagon down a six-lane interstate. The tolls are mounting up. Debs directs from memory, from intuition, from a 1964 road map of America she finds in the glove compartment.

"Get off here," she says.

"Here?" Ditch asks. He can't believe it.

The next thing you know, they'll be home.

It's raining.

Ditch tries to stop it, feels it coming like a handclap. He stumbles, opens his eyes. Houses orbit past, green lawns splayed. His wet knees in someone's grass. He's holding his ears. Maryland, he thinks.

Merryland.

Earthquake.

His big hands covering his ears.

"We can walk from here," Debs announces. She hesitates, touches him lightly on the shoulder. He gets up, staggers a few steps, falls. His head hits a fire hydrant.

"Bobby! Bobby!"

Debs stands over him. Looking down.

"Are you okay?" she asks.

He drags himself to his hands, his knees. It all seems so simple: get up. Just get up. Only we don't know who we are.

Debs touches the top of his head. Pulls him into her.

Treasure the Chesapeake emblazoned on a licence plate. Cars to bridges over water. Windsurfers strapped on roofs, cappuccino in styrofoam, a parking lot far from home.

Ditch gets to his feet, steadies himself on the hot hood of the wagon, the engine still creaking and groaning.

"It's out of gas," Debs explains. "We'll walk from here."

"Who's Bobby? I'm not Bobby?"

"What are you talking about?" She looks at him, disgusted.

He peers past a verdant lawn. Property demarcated by mowing stripes. A face between curtains. Looks familiar to him, looks at him. He's never been here before. Red brick. Half-peeled curtains. A knowing smile. Ditch blinks and can't seem to see anything.

Spying on them.

Debs dabs at his head with a fast-food napkin. Blood comes off, wet fire-hydrant rust.

"You're bleeding," she says, shaking her head. "Come on. Quit fooling around. They're expecting us."

"They're expecting us?"

She just looks at him.

"I'm not...I wasn't," he tells her. He shakes his head. "Just a cramp in my leg, all that driving." He puts his hands on his forehead. Presses down. A deliberate agony, satisfying, like bursting a pimple. He laughs anyway, makes a big show of looking around. "So are we here? Is this it? This is... nice. Quiet."

"Didn't you hear me? We have to go."

The air is golden, sun through diminishing clouds. Shadows slip behind backyard trees, an impoverished lustre, a pale shine. What could they do, anyway? What did he think they could do? She takes his hand. The distance between us. *I mean, okay, what's the worst that could happen?*

(He still dreams about it. About what really happened.)

"This is it," she says after a while. "I guess this is it."

He knows what she means. Her grip tightens to hold on.

"For a while this piano teacher used to come to the house. He stank of wine, you could smell it on him. He was from some crazy place, I don't know, Bulgaria or Bolivia. He always wore the same brown suit and under it a pleated white shirt. I don't know where the hell they found him. You should have seen his teeth. I guess they don't have orthodontists in Bulgaria. I never had to go to the orthodontist. My teeth are straight, see? He didn't teach me anything. He would stand over me and I would feel his breath on the back of my head."

And Ditch: "You live on Devilwood? This is your street? It's actually called Devilwood?"

The houses expand, extra guest rooms, elaborate marble baths, smoky dens and leathery cigar lounges. The lawns more luxurious, the shrubbery behind the pool increasingly ornate. Finished basements, hollow empty caverns deep under the earth.

"Do you think we're too late?" Ditch says. "It's so quiet."

"Too late?" Debs seems surprised. "There's plenty of time."

She keeps talking, like a teenager on the phone with her new boyfriend after their first fight.

Ditch tries to stop himself, walks into dizzy scenery, everything still a highway blur.

They pass bushes in topiary shapes. Japanese cherry trees inexplicably in full bloom. It seems to Ditch that he's walked down this quiet summer street a thousand times. A thousand thousand times.

But they aren't getting anywhere.

Debs is smiling — a fat grin, glazed bright — lipstick — Where did she?

Party dress perfect mouth, her hair tousled. Bent. He wants to stop, pull her against him, make her beauty real. He puts his hands over his eyes. The world cracks. Debs spills laughter everywhere, wet rain, nothing for something.

Sometime later Ditch will have to explain:

"There was never anything between us. I mean, the way she was with me was the way she was with everyone. I'm not saying we didn't sleep together. And I'm not saying she slept with everyone, either. Don't get me wrong. She wasn't a — Look, you want to know what she is? I can't tell you. I don't think there is anyone in the world who could tell you. Maybe her father. Maybe him. I don't know. I never met him. Maybe he knows. Wherever he is. If he's even — He might be able to tell you. I never really wanted to know, you know? Don't you get it? What I wanted to know she couldn't tell me. You have to understand — it was a — it was a difficult — period. I wasn't thinking straight, all the stuff we did, after a while I didn't need to know. You get it? I was afraid to know. Her eyes. She kept telling me — like mirrors. We weren't on drugs or anything. She didn't kill anybody. You have to understand, you can't just — She isn't crazy. How is she? Tell her I say hi. Tell her I —"

The halls in the basement are twice as wide as the rest of the house. They are poorly lit, bulbs embedded deep in the ceiling so that each step forward moves them into another fading circle. It's easy to get lost, the corridors meet each other, all the carpets are the same dark red, all the walls are the same sepia brown.

This is what Ditch knows: that the basement extends beyond the boundaries of the house, transgresses the white wood fences staking out property, breaks all the rules.

Metal rails line the walls, pipes painted a liquid white. The bars and railings and handholds are the fuselage of some giant entwining plant, roots writhing in the walls, occasionally bursting through to proffer a contorted limb. Ditch avoids the bars, keeps his arms tight to his sides as he walks. The random banisters can be followed to a central chamber bigger than all the rest. The locus of this room — shaped, like all the rooms, in a perfect square — is the bed. The bed is fenced in.

Ditch pictures hospitals, detox centres, retards and maniacs and addicts tied down for their own good. A length of rail is already lowered, leaving that long side open and inviting: *Come rest here. Just a little nap. Warm, you know. Comfortable.*

And it *is* cold in the basement. His muscles contort, twitch a warning. He wants to run, put his feet down on the gas pedal, follow the route. There isn't a route. She pulls back the soft duvet slowly, showing sheets, white like clouds. She steps away. The bed's in the locked position, the rails up. At the foot of the bed is the control panel. A lever to raise the front half of the bed, another to lower the rear half, a switch to release the locks on the railings. The buttons are orange. He hears air like a rush of panicked animals. Debs strokes his face tenderly, as if explaining something very carefully to someone who won't ever understand.

What's down there, Mommy?
Nothing, dear.

We visit the meat-packing plant. The Parent does it with the foreman in his office. I slip past dangling slabs of beef. Into the rows of killing stalls, the metal clamps and leather braces hanging empty. I stand where they trap the animal, head in a truss, bolt slamming through the skull. I trail a hand through my hair, thin and greasy. I can feel my brain bulging under my soft scalp. What's it like, do you think, Daddy? The smell isn't that bad. Fear and sawdust. In the distance, I can hear soft hot breathing, the shuffle of hooves. So what? My hand moves down, along the side of my neck, through my tiny tits. I bunch up my skirt, dig a finger in.

She likes it here, the Parent says when they finally find me, asleep, curled up on the drain, stainless steel speckled with flecks of bloody rust. The Parent's smeared lipstick mouth. The beefy fellow trailing behind, tucking his undershirt into his trousers.

She points the cursor to a favourite picture. A woman half twisted on her side, legs open, the shot from a high angle so that Ditch can see her filled with dick, and he can see her small tight breasts and the white teeth that line the inside of her cute cheerleader smile.

"She looks like me."

"Jesus."

He feels faint. He feels himself on his own, out of control. He puts his hand on her shoulder, touches her, again, or else for the first time; a surprise: how soft and thin she is; the girl he thought he knew.

She thinks about licking his nipples. He touches her. She leans into him, his emptiness.

He's her first victim.

She was right about me, he thinks.

Debs checks the lock on the door leading down. She turns and leans against it. For a moment, she hears the perfect virgin silence.

Bobby opens me up on the hospital bed. It's my first time, Daddy. My fingers curl around the rails, locked into place. His sperm and my blood trickle down my thighs and through the pristine sheets. (Will I bleed? I'll know what it's like. Imprisoned, pinioned, allowed everything. I'll bleed.)

But he doesn't want her any more. Her smell fills the empty spaces of the house, and he can't get away. Or else it's the way her flesh clings to him when he touches her. He doesn't know how it happens.

It happens like this:

She leads him to the door of the basement, kisses him, presses against him, flattens him. He feels dizzy, hears his heart beating in his mouth. When he tries to speak, the saliva rushes out and coats his chin. He closes his eyes to stop the spiral from pulling him down. She straps him in and sits on his face. Sighs. The basement: at peace with its own suffocating principle.

"Down here," she says. Her hands around his neck.

"Jesus," he tries to say.

He thought, many years later, that he could have gotten away from her, that maybe he did get away from her. Years later he thinks: Where were her parents? And then: What happened to me?

He tells himself that he should try to stop her. He tells himself that what's done is done, that it's too late.

I'm not crazy. She's the one who's crazy.

Anyway, he can't move. Or he can move, but he's forgotten how. It's too late, isn't it?

She isn't beautiful any more. He tries to pull away from her. They go downstairs. She holds his hand, her arm trailing behind her, towing him.

"Dark," she says.

He remembers her saying that. He remembers the gloom. He remembers hearing a pounding on the door — someone knocking — we'll have to stop now. But she's working at the buttons of his jeans. The bed groans. They lower themselves in. He can't move.

He tries to scream.

Her smooth fingers in his mouth. The silence. The old sheet smell, sterile sickness over them. Upstairs a dull thud, like a cell door closing.

"What was that? Was that the door? Is somebody locking us in?"

Her tongue gagging him.

The furnace shifts to life.

I close my eyes. I open them. I imagine the sun is about to rise and the graying of the screen is beginning and I will see everything. It's like when I was a little girl and we were staying at the ocean and I would wake up early early and see the whole big blue sky and the sun just creeping over the sand. At three o'clock in the morning in the empty living room I spread my legs. I keep my eyes on the screen of the laptop. I shudder. I blink.

One night, Debs reads to him. Her voice creeps out of the shadows: a glance, a graze. All the fear is gone. He can feel his dick swelling, separating from his body. He can't feel anything.

"She was the only child, though she wasn't a child any more. She had no friends, there was a boy, well, some kind of a man. Bobby told his pals she wasn't as crazy as she seemed and that they should stop being such assholes and fuck off and not give him a hard time about it. Anyway, they were just jealous 'cause he was maybe getting some. And anyway, it wasn't serious. It wasn't like he was going out with her. Girl like that. From a family like that, her father, if it's true what they say, or else they're just — Bobby hasn't even met her father."

Ditch struggles to listen; it's important, he tells himself. The room spins. Desperately, he tries to pump his crotch.

"Of course he was just waiting to go to college in another state. And to himself he admitted she was weirder than even they thought; there was something about her: small pointed breasts; pale milky eyes; he was always saying: 'Why are you looking at me like that?' There was something about her that he could not deny. Dancing in the silence of the long dark basement, she suddenly pushed him away. She pulled off her sweatshirt. Her tits glistening. Her chest heaving.

"He was trying, always trying to kiss her, in between everything else there was for her his anxious boy breath, and her not saying much about it.

"One week she jerked him off. She didn't take it out though. She did it through his jeans.

"The next week she couldn't imagine touching him. She looked out from behind the front room's thick curtains and pictured him peering back at her. That was after everyone was already gone. Just the girl left, alone. The house was carpeted, air-conditioned, protected by an alarm system she didn't know how to use. Everyone was gone. Except for Bobby."

Sunday afternoon. Barbara puts away the groceries. She buys less now that Ditch is —

Standing there in the kitchen, interrupted gestures, carton of milk in her hand.

Still afternoons. Everything sounds soft and distant, like a promise.

A car with a bad muffler, wheezing by.

The gurgle of the pipes.

The neighbours, yelling at each other in a mix of English and Portuguese.

Somewhere, in some other world, a dog barks furiously and an owner says, "Oh, stop it, Missy."

The silence is a filter, separating each distant effect into separate parts. I'm all right, Barbara tells her friends at work. She means it. She really does.

A tap on the front door. Barbara shakes her head, comes back to herself, stores the milk in its slot in the refrigerator.

The knock again, louder this time.

She makes her way through the hall, expecting a Jehovah's Witness or a college kid with a petition selling a Save the Whales calendar.

(But who does she really suspect? Two police detectives — one tall, one short — bearing bad news about the son she refuses to think about? Or the drunken ex-husband who left her when the son was five? Or will it be the girl, her angel face smeared with blood?)

The man at the door is tall, old, grandiose, encumbered with a style you don't see any more. She stares at his pencil moustache, at the protruding bulb of his nose.

She knows him, she knows all about him.

"I'm sorry," she finally says. "Can I — Do I know you?"

"I'm Aaron Knudtsen. I'm the brother of your...former boarder."

"Yes, of course you are!" Barbara exclaims. She feels like she has to pretend. "I didn't recognize you at first — but then I thought I had seen you before. Just that once, at the funeral."

The man on the step — Aaron Knudtsen — shifts uncomfortably in his black trench coat.

"How rude of me!" Barbara cries. "Please, won't you come in! Do come in."

"I would hate to impose."

"Nonsense! You must come in. I was just about to make coffee."

Barbara hears herself laugh. She doesn't feel empty, she doesn't feel like she's missing something. The sound is a trilling anger, as if a bad smell could be covered up with proper etiquette, with the right spray of perfume. She should slap him. Slam the door in his face.

It isn't his fault. Nothing is anybody's fault.

Aaron follows her in, lets her take his hat and gloves, his coat. He's carrying an attaché case, which gives him the air of a retired noble.

He sits stiffly at the table, doesn't speak. She makes coffee, puts fancy biscuits on a fancy plate.

"Please excuse the mess," she says of the spotless kitchen. "I wasn't expecting company."

"I'm imposing," Aaron says.

She knows she's overdoing it. But she can't help herself.

"Milk?" she says. "Or cream? Oh dear, I don't have any cream. Sugar?" She flits around him.

"Please," Aaron says. "If you'll just...join me..."

She takes a seat at the table. Neither of them speaks, then both start at once.

"I came here —"

"We didn't —"

"Please —" Aaron says, indicating that she should proceed. Barbara flushes.

"It's only that, well, myself and my son — we didn't know Maury had a brother."

"Well he did," Aaron says. "At the time I was...away."

"Travelling?" Barbara says brightly. She hates him. She's acting her role. Aggrieved mother. Widow who never even had a husband. Is he alone in the world? Is that the way she sees her? Is that what this is about?

"No, well," Aaron Knudtsen shakes his head. "Maury and

I, we were..."

He opens the briefcase, pulls out a photo album.

"I thought you might like to have these. They were Maury's pictures. I made duplicates."

"How kind of you!" Barbara takes the leather album, feels its weight. "And it's so beautiful."

"Thank you."

They stare down at their cups. The dark trapped liquid undulating. Hints of steam.

"Well," Barbara breathes. "Should I look at them now?"

"Please, do."

She lifts the heavy lid. Inside, porous photos of young men, black-and-white poses from another country. Another century.

"The first pages are from our days in the shtetl. That's me, and there is Maury."

"How handsome you were. Such young gentlemen. But so serious."

"Yes. Those were...different times. The young people today — "

"What about them?"

Aaron Knudtsen frowns. She can see his fingers, withered, yet perfectly manicured.

"It's just that..." he says, "those were different times."

"Yes. That's true. I suppose they were — No. That isn't true. I don't suppose things were all that different, even then. Did you ever think, Mr. Knudtsen, that things weren't so different, after all? You know, Maury never talked about his family. He never showed me any pictures. Then he passed away. And I found out he had a brother, and I asked Ditch — my son — to send his things over to you. I shouldn't have, my son, he was dealing with his own...so I shouldn't have...but, at the time, I couldn't face it myself."

Barbara flips through several pages as she talks, the images blurring by, bleak monotones, smiling young men and women, stern-looking elders in black. She wants to explain something to him. Something about absence and family and the way she recognizes herself — her flawed desperate propriety — in his polished nails and starched collars. She pauses on a page with a single shot: a powerful-looking woman grimacing at the camera, clearly uninterested in the distraction of photography.

"Our mother."

"Of course," Barbara says. "She looks very...formidable."

Aaron Knudtsen's short laugh startles her. A bird shooting out of long grass.

"But, please," he says. "Continue. I believe the other pictures will be more...familiar."

Ditch's tenth birthday.

Trips to the zoo, to the Chinese restaurant. Maury sitting at the kitchen table, helping Ditch with his homework.

Maury's seventieth.

Barbara looks up at her visitor, sees him sitting there.

"These are absolutely..." she says. "I didn't even realize he had these."

"You were his family," Aaron says.

Barbara nods.

"I..." Aaron says, his voice fumbling. "I regret certain outcomes. The falling out — my brother and me."

Barbara takes his hand.

"Come and see me again," she says.

Ditch blinks. There's a banner over the glass screen doors, sun pouring in, a bright red crab dancing in front of a computer, claws working the keys. Crustacean eyes almost touching the caricature of a busty naked girl writhing on top of the monitor.

WWW.CRABGIRLS.COM

"So I said to him, let's get one thing straight. I'm the goddamn boss. If anyone's gonna fuck one of my girls, it's gonna be me."

A woman in a maid outfit more fetish than functional stoops down to offer him her breasts, a freckled slope, champagne in fluted crystal.

"How's the party going?" Ditch says, surprised to hear his own voice, so calm and hard. The woman giggles, blushes. Ditch watches his fingers squeeze, the thin glass is weak, permeable.

Only it's impossibly bright. Summertime.

"Are you a crab girl?"

She smiles a few angled teeth, *find out for yourself...*

Ditch follows her pointing red claw. He sees the adjacent dining room, lights off, dim blue glow, the long table supporting a row of terminals. There's a buzzing noise he suddenly can't stop hearing. It fills the house, empty despite the crowd of guests. It's the hive of unstoppable industry, activity continual and inescapable, a kind of life, a kind of memory. Never closes! Open 24 hours! He drinks champagne.

A skeletal hand digs into his shoulder. The same voice as before — skinny and nervous, insistent in its awkwardness, the proprietor of some terrible silence — *if anybody's gonna fuck my girls...* Ditch raises his head, remembers what death looks like — Morts. The man's face is flushed from drinking. The blank emerald eyes sparked with gold. Ditch recognizes them the way he seems to recognize everything.

The porn king.

"Well, I'm glad you could make it. I know Debs thinks a lot of you. I'm just glad the two of you could make it. Where you from again? Well, it doesn't matter. The important thing is that she wanted you here. And here you are! If I were you I wouldn't disappoint her. She's a fine girl, I love her to death, that girl. Hey, get yourself a bucket of crabs. Don't just sit there! Try our famous drink — the Black-Eyed Suzie."

Cold flesh, bone through bone.

"Yes, sir," Ditch says casually. "Debs sure is a fine girl. Now if only I knew where she took off to..."

A frown on the father's face. He tilts his head. His ethereal throat twisting around a lump of liquor. He looks suddenly lost.

"Now, you don't worry about that. She'll be back soon. She's just in the basement with her mother. Those two.

They're a lot alike if you ask me. Anyway, they'll be down there getting reacquainted. You don't want to disturb her down there. You know how those women are — ha — go get yourself some crabs — Babs! How wonderful you came! Have you seen the new site?"

Ditch watches him operate, his gaunt lips pecking the cheek off a plump matron, silver Mercedes, a husband who fears her, a power she doesn't mind using. So much money, Ditch thinks, and my mother can't even afford a car. It's possible that whatever happens next doesn't happen. Even so, Ditch will always remember the way the porn king seemed like all the dead men in his life — a natural disaster, a victim of love.

He swallows a Black-Eyed Suzie, bright yellow drink under ice, makes his teeth ache, he doesn't taste it, drinks it down. Throws the glass in a fireplace big enough for a pig roast. A smattering of applause. He looks around for another. "Best not to disturb them," he whispers. "You know how women are." There's the buzz on his head, the muted roar of distant machinery, and a smell of rot. Like everything, it's just so damn familiar. In a few years — or is that days and months? — the mother will drive the father crazy, he'll raise his hand to her. An accident. There's a daughter too, he's sure of that.

Everything is brighter than it is. Outside on the deck, girls in bikinis and chef's hats are boiling huge pots of fat crabs. Men and women with double chins and dyed hair wear *CRABGIRLS.COM* aprons over their formal outfits. They sit at picnic tables covered in newspapers and suck the meat out of claws, juicy lips pursed. Ditch inhales decay like impending weather. People giggle softly and speak confidently to their neighbours on matters of high finance. They have the air of corrupt officials. They dip morsels of meat in vinegar or melted butter.

"I'm Bobby," he tells the couple across from him. "Friend of the family." His fingers know what to do. Fresh crab from the Chesapeake. His favourite. *But I've never* — He wields a wooden mallet, takes a deep humid breath, lets hot air soak into his lungs. He finds the tab on the underside, peels the exoskeleton. Drops the hammer on the casing of a fat claw. Butter drips down his chin.

"Can I take your shells?" his waitress asks. He grabs her with a greasy hand. He pulls her into the dining room. Shrouded terminals. Blue list of options. The sound is loud in here. He is sitting, she is over him, wrapped around like a fur. He looks down. His legs are gone. The keyboard stretches, covers everything. He doesn't know where he is. Calmly, he types in a string of letters and symbols.

"She made me memorize it," he says. "In case." The waitress clucks sympathetically. The screen fills. A bright house. Limos in the circular driveway getting bigger then disappearing as the view hones in.

"That's us," the waitress squeals. Ditch kisses her. She straddles the keyboard.

Debs hasn't ever wanted anything.

Nothing happens. She graduates high school, lets her quarterback boyfriend have her for the first time, prom night, a limo and a pink corsage, French restaurant, jug of tequila procured courtesy someone's older brother.

She's still in high school. She'll always be in high school.

It's their fault —

The Parent —

Daddy,

— he isn't here. He isn't anywhere.

They gave her ballet and horseback and painting and swimming and Italian and piano and skating lessons.

In the basement there are no mirrors and she doesn't have to see herself. She'd like to break something. She'd like to smash up the place. That isn't nice, dear. Who would stop her? Who would grab her wrists and hold her body? She imagines trembling against herself, collapsing and crying.

It's okay now, dear.

And realizing the error of her ways. And applying herself to the project of making something of her future.

There's no one to tell her what to do.

Nobody, Debs thinks, feeling sorry for herself.

So what? I'm —

She's the last girl on earth, free to be absolutely —

alone.

I'm not!

She'll scream at him, sometimes. She's disappearing. How do you like it? she'll scream. How do you like my disappearing act?

He's her new boyfriend. Maybe this time, she'll go all the way.

So far, she hasn't. She just glides her body against his, snuggles up. All of this, not what happened exactly; not exactly what she wanted to happen. She wanted it to be perfect, for once, for a change, is that too much to ask? But it didn't work out that way. Look at yourself. Look around you. To her, it looks like a picture in an old man's album: fading, pointless.

The thing she pictured was perfect.

She opens the laptop. An arc of light swallowed by the basement gloom. Behind her, sheets rustle against his muffled limbs. The sound is a comfort to her. Proximity like memory; the smell of Daddy after he shaves, aftershave, before he goes out, pink cheeks, slapped cheeks. Take me with you.

Isn't that nice, dear.

Debs logs on, enters the requisite codes and passwords and indicators.

The pictures hang in the dark amber of the underworld, archaeological anomalies preserved long after their time.

That isn't me.

Who is it?

One by one, she deletes them.

In his bed where he lies ill, where she nurses him until he's all the way better, he tries to turn to the pale light, the cords in his neck popping.

The site is empty. She leaves a single snapshot.

— *take pictures of me* —

Grey blot patterns. Look close. Press your nose against the screen. What do you see? What's the first thing that comes into your head?

The outline of the bathtub? The blurred swing of a slim ankle ending in a shaking foot? Toes point to the descending night.

Debs thinks of her fans, her admirers, her would-be stalkers. They'll keep coming back. Two, three, four years later. They'll remember me. That isn't — She's in there for real, boys, for forever

— a ghost, she thinks.

Groans from the hospital bed.

He's tied to the rails. Debs on his chest. Her lips bloody. Red marking the flat space between his nipples. Someone hammering on the door, the distant thud flooding through the long hallways, a sound as irrepressible as the real world. Debs is crying, licking the plains of his face like a thirsty cat.

"Please, wake up," she begs. "Wake up. We don't have much time. I was waiting for you. I've been waiting for you."

Reluctantly, he opens his eyes — the quiet an echo. Nothing under it. The bed cradles his body. He tries to move, he can't move. I'm locked, he thinks, somehow relieved. He imagines himself as a door. Leading back into nowhere. There's blood on his face. Or something else wet. Knudtsen's short rumpled body slipping under the newspaper tide with a rustle. He thinks of his mother then, her loneliness, the wonderful futility of her smile, the way she says his name. You're just a promise. A picture for a wallet you can't seem to stop losing. He can hardly breathe. He doesn't want to have to breathe.

When he opens his eyes again, he sees her like a shadow, like what's lost. She can't take it back, it's over

— *it's what we don't know, my father* —

Ditch won't see him again.

Debs holds on.

"You're just a kid," he says. "Fuck, Debs, you're just —"

He slips his wrists out. He puts his arms around her quaking body.

"What is your mother like?"

He licks his lips. Laughs. When they want to hear, they hear. They tape-record everything. As if someone's going to forget. Does she get the letters? Does she write to him?

"She's a wonderful woman."

"What is she like?"

He smiles. He feels himself smiling.

"I never knew her."

Barbara picks him up from the bus station.

She doesn't cry.

"Ditch. Ditch. Oh, Ditch, baby."

She wants it to be true. And he wants to tell her: *Nothing happened. It's all the same. I'm the same. Nothing happened.*

He plays with the ripped ticket, his hand in his jeans pocket. He's been fingering the tattered paper all the way from San Francisco. "I'm sorry," he says instead. "I'll pay you back."

"Do you think you can?"

That's when she cries.

They walk away from the bus station, into the city he never really left.

"Here," she says, touching his shoulder.

"Hey," he says, "you didn't tell me...you finally did it. You did it."

"It's not new," she says.

He kicks a tire. "But it's great," he says. "It's like new."

Barbara laughs. She drives him home. He's a stranger now.

She unlocks the door, doesn't want her hands to shake. Her hands shake. It's been happening lately. It just happens. Nothing to do with —

The dark foyer still smells of his boots. And something else, a shadow of sweat and perfume, crumpled leaves, though it's not fall, though it hasn't been fall for a long time.

"Mom, I —"

"Just don't," she says.

She goes inside.

He takes his hands out of his pockets.

"Can you believe this place?"

"You need a trail of bread crumbs just to find your way out."

"Blood, in this house."

"Blood crumbs."

"Ha ha. Yeah."

The two detectives drag Ditch through the gloom of recessed lights. Bare feet trailing on soft carpet. The one man is short, thin, wizened. He wears gloves, but his grip is pincer-sharp. The other is tall, abundant, his soft hand gentle under Ditch's armpit.

"This one doesn't weigh much."

"Wonder what his story is."

"Been down here for a while. Was down here when it happened, I bet."

"You think he helped out?"

"He's in rough shape."

"They'll fix him up."

"Oh yeah, the miracles of modern science."

"Then we'll see."

"He'll talk."

"Sure, he'll talk."

"He won't know anything."

"No, he doesn't know anything."

Acknowledgements

Parts of *Ditch* first appeared in *Exile* and *B&A: new fiction.*

Thanks to the MacDowell Colony for giving me a place to write and think, and thanks to the Canada Council for the Arts for helping me get there.

I'm grateful to all those who read and commented on various incarnations of this book. First and foremost, Ken Sparling, who possesses a rare mix of talent and boundless patience; and also, Emily Pohl-Weary, Chris Frey, Rachel Cohen and Hilary Clark for their valuable input.

My editor Anne Collins brought both unflagging enthusiasm and keen insight to the publication of this novel.

Finally, appreciation to my agent Bruce Westwood, and gratitude to my family — kids, dog and sisters-in-law included.